You've Found Oliver

Praise for Dustin Thao:

You've Reached Sam

'I am here to warn you: This book will absolutely make you cry. Make sure you've got a box of tissues handy, and I mean a full box' NPR

'*You've Reached Sam* is a hauntingly remarkable debut. Dustin Thao gently weaves grief, regret, second chances, and the honestly beautiful moments we carry from a first love. Every tear you will shed reading this book will be worth it.' Julian Winters, award-winning author of *Running With Lions*

'Have your tissues at the ready when you dive into Dustin Thao's emotional novel *You've Reached Sam*' PopSugar

'*You've Reached Sam* is a quiet exploration of grief and the ways in which we cope with losing the ones we love too soon. If you're in need of a good, cathartic crying session, this one's for you!' The Nerd Daily

When Haru Was Here

'I read *When Haru Was Here* in a single sitting, and cried at the ending. Filled with raw emotions, relatable moments, and a touch of enchantment, prepare to have your heart broken and mended by the time the story is over.' Alex Aster, No. 1 *New York Times*-bestselling author of *Lightlark*

'*When Haru Was Here* is a mind-bending, gut-punching, heart-healing portrait of grief. It's magical how Dustin Thao can make you fall in love with having your heart broken.' Adam Silvera, No. 1 *New York Times*-bestselling author of *They Both Die at the End*

'Thao casts an intelligent look into the harm and benefits of one teen's coping mechanisms in this sharply depicted exploration of grief and moving on' *Publishers Weekly*

'Devastatingly honest and achingly human, *When Haru Was Here* is a melodic exploration of love, loneliness, and the multitude of ways grief shapes us. No one captures the beauty in heartbreak like Dustin Thao.' Julian Winters, award-winning author of *Right Where I Left You*

Also by Dustin Thao

You've Reached Sam

When Haru Was Here

You've Found Oliver

DUSTIN THAO

FIRST INK

First published 2025 in the US by Dutton Books, an imprint of Penguin Random House LLC

First published 2025 in the UK by First Ink,
an imprint of Pan Macmillan
The Smithson, 6 Briset Street, London EC1M 5NR
EU representative: Macmillan Publishers Ireland Ltd, 1st Floor,
The Liffey Trust Centre, 117–126 Sheriff Street Upper, Dublin 1 D01 YC43
Associated companies throughout the world

ISBN 978-1-0350-5243-1

Copyright © Dustin Thao 2025

The right of Dustin Thao to be identified as the author of this work has been
asserted in accordance with the Copyright, Designs and Patents Act 1988.

The epigraph on p. ix is from *The Poetics of Space* by Gaston Bachelard
(France: Presses Universitaires de France, 1958).

All rights reserved. No part of this publication may be reproduced,
stored in a retrieval system, or transmitted, in any form, or by any means
(including, without limitation, electronic, mechanical, photocopying, recording
or otherwise) without the prior written permission of the publisher.

Pan Macmillan does not have any control over, or any responsibility for,
any author or third-party websites (including, without limitation, URLs,
emails and QR codes) referred to in or on this book.

1 3 5 7 9 8 6 4 2

A CIP catalogue record for this book is available from the British Library.

Printed and bound in the UK using 100% Renewable Electricity by CPI Group (UK) Ltd
Design by Anna Booth

This book is sold subject to the condition that it shall not, by way of trade or otherwise,
be lent, hired out, or otherwise circulated without the publisher's prior consent in any
form of binding or cover other than that in which it is published and without a similar
condition including this condition being imposed on the subsequent purchaser.
The publisher does not authorize the use or reproduction of any part of this book in
any manner for the purpose of training artificial intelligence technologies or systems.
The publisher expressly reserves this book from the Text and Data Mining exception in
accordance with Article 4(3) of the European Union Digital Single Market Directive 2019/790.

Visit **www.panmacmillan.com** to read more about all our books and buy them.

For Alex Aster & Chloe Gong,
who showed up to the wrong restaurant
and inspired this story

"The imagination separates us from the past as well as from reality; it faces the future."

—Gaston Bachelard, *The Poetics of Space*

PROLOGUE

BEFORE

After all this time, I still think about him.

It feels like yesterday when he was here. Sunlight flickers through the branches as I open my eyes. I'm lying out in the grass, hands resting on my stomach. A few petals fall from the sky as I turn my head slowly. Sam is sitting there beside me with a notebook in his lap. And suddenly, it's the spring of freshman year again.

"Enjoy your nap?" he asks.

I close my eyes again. "I wasn't napping."

"Oh, *really*?"

"I'm just resting my eyes."

"For forty minutes? Well, the snoring was a nice touch."

"*Forty minutes?*" I blink at him. "Jesus, why didn't you wake me up?"

"I thought you were *resting your eyes*," Sam says, smirking a little. He pushes himself up, setting his pencil on the grass. "I actually just lost track of time. Had to finish my drawing." A breeze comes, gently ruffling his dark hair. I could lie out here all day, watching him. "It's looking pretty good, too."

"What about the math assignment?"

He winces. "I forgot about that..."

"Sam, it's due tomorrow! Who am I supposed to copy off?"

"You don't want to see my drawing?" He glances at me. "It's of you."

I narrow my eyes. "*Show me...*"

Sam hands me his notebook. There's a sketch of me, lying in the grass with one hand behind my head, surrounded by flowers. I've never had anyone draw me before.

"I'm not the best at shadows," he says.

"You did this while I was sleeping?"

"You can tell me if you hate it."

"I mean, it's not *bad*." I point at myself in the drawing. "But you got the arms wrong. My muscles are much more defined."

Sam rubs his chin. "I knew something was off..."

We both laugh. I hand him back the notebook. "I like the flowers you added. Roses, right?"

"White roses. Those are my favorite."

"Mine too," I say. To be honest, I didn't have a favorite flower before. But that's what it is now.

"You know what I've been thinking about?" says Sam. "Guys don't get enough flowers."

"*Agreed*. Society needs to change."

Sam smiles. There's a silence before he says, "Can I ask you something?"

"Shoot."

"Who's Zach?"

The name catches me by surprise. How does he know about Zach?

Sam glances at my phone, which is between us. "Sorry, I noticed he texted you a few times."

"He's a friend," I say, vaguely.

"How come we haven't met yet?"

"He lives all the way in Redmond." It's another small town in Washington, right outside of Seattle, about an hour and a half away from Ellensburg.

"Cool. How long have you known him?"

I run my hand over the grass, not wanting to answer. "I don't know. Not that long." We've only been talking for a few weeks. I haven't even met him in person yet. And I'm too embarrassed to mention this. Especially when I'm not exactly out at school yet.

"You know you can tell me anything," he says.

I hesitate. Sam and I have been best friends since seventh grade. We know pretty much everything about each other. But there are a few things I'm not ready to share yet. "I know . . ." is all I say.

Sam offers another smile. Then he stares out at the lake. "The water looks nice today," he says, changing the subject for me. "Maybe we should go for a swim."

I scoff. "And put off our homework?"

He lets out a breath. "You're right. We have to be responsible."

We both narrow our eyes, looking at each other. There's this game we play sometimes. I wait for the smirk to rise on Sam's face, and then we both jump to our feet. The next thing I know, we're racing toward the dock, shirts thrown behind us. The second we crash into the water, everything around us vanishes as the memory changes . . .

Dress shoes slap on marble floors of the hotel lobby. Sam and I are standing outside the ballroom, wearing button-up shirts and bow ties. Music pours out through the double doors as Sam sticks his head in and says, "Are you sure this is a good idea?"

"What's the worst that could happen?"

"We get arrested."

"For crashing a wedding?"

Sam sighs. "I don't know how you talk me into this stuff."

It's the fall of sophomore year. The Sagamore is the nicest hotel in Ellensburg. We've walked past it a hundred times and joked about sneaking in someday. To be completely honest, I never thought we'd actually do it, but here we are. I clasp Sam's shoulders and say, "We'll go in, grab a slice of cake, and go. Maybe a drink or two. No one will ever know we were here."

"I hope there's shrimp cocktail."

"That's the spirit."

We adjust each other's collars before heading inside. Flowers fill the entrance as we make our way toward the crowd of wedding guests. You know these people have money because the ice sculptures are bigger than both of us. I reach out to touch one of the ice swans.

Sam shoves me. *"Stop that."*

"I was checking if it was real."

"We're supposed to be invisible, remember?" Sam shakes his head at me. Then he glances around the room and says, "Wait a minute. Is that a photo booth?"

"A *photo booth?*"

We race over to it. Several pictures later, we grab our prints and head toward the buffet to get some food. Sam's face lights up at the chocolate-covered strawberries. He places two on his plate and says, "Everything looks *so good.*"

"Told you this was a great idea."

"Could you imagine having a wedding like this?"

I shrug. "It's a bit much, if you ask me."

"But you want to get married, right?"

I think about this. "Maybe. Do you?"

"Of course. I mean, if I meet the right person." His eyes move around the room as if he's imagining it for himself. "Doesn't have to be *this* extravagant though."

"I guess weddings are a good way to get flowers," I say.

"True." Sam smiles, turning back to the dessert.

I wish I could tell him how handsome he looks tonight. How the light around us brings out the deep brown in his eyes. We find a table and enjoy our food. Then we wander toward the dance floor to see the band. As we're enjoying the music, a tall man approaches us.

"Excuse me," he says. "I don't think I've seen you boys before."

Sam and I exchange a nervous glance. Before either of us can speak, the guy behind him with a camera says, "Do you have a few words for the bride and groom?"

We blink at each other. Sam nudges me.

"*Uh . . . of course,*" I start. I put my arm around Sam and smile into the camera. "Thank you for sharing this *beautiful* night with us. I think I speak for everyone when I say, you two are truly made for each other. Watching you fall in love over the years was a gift to us all. So congratulations to . . . uh—" I freeze, realizing I don't know their names.

"*You lovebirds!*" Sam jumps in to save me.

"Stop, I'm getting emotional," I add, fanning my eyes.

The moment the man turns away, Sam grabs my arm. I'm laughing as he pulls me aside, looking worried all of a sudden. "Oliver, I think it's time to go.".

"But they haven't even cut the cake!"

"I don't want us to get caught."

"Relax, nobody's noticed yet."

"We've stayed long enough," he says firmly. "I'm gonna grab my jacket and meet you at the door."

"*Boo.*"

He walks off before I can stop him. The music was just getting good, too. As I'm standing there, not yet ready to leave, an idea comes to me. I head up to the band and make a request. Thankfully, the guitarist knows the song. As I'm waiting for them to play it, Sam returns to the dance floor and says, "What's taking so long? You were supposed to meet me by the door."

"How about one more song?" I suggest.

"*You* can stay for one more song. I'm gonna wait in the car."

"*Come on, Sammy.*" I grab his arm.

But he pulls away. "I'll be outside."

I stand there as Sam begins to walk off again. Then, as if on cue, there's a familiar drum intro. He pauses, recognizing the beat instantly. There's only one song that could get Sam to stay. "Escape," by Rupert Holmes, better known as "The Piña Colada Song." It's unironically one of Sam's favorites of all time. He's forced me to listen to it a thousand times in the car. We choreographed a dance to it for his parents' anniversary a few years back.

Sam turns around slowly, narrowing his eyes at me. I smile as I step toward him, rolling my shoulders to the beat. Eventually, Sam taps his foot as if the music's taken over. The moment the chorus hits, he finally surrenders to it, dancing along with me. To my surprise, we remember the moves almost perfectly. I love seeing him like this, singing along to the words, as if no one around is watching us.

Haze blankets us, pouring down from a fog machine on the stage. Sam shuffles toward it, making me follow after him. The music fades as we disappear through the fog, and the memory changes once again . . .

Fog turns to mist as I step off the city bus. It's seven-thirty on a Saturday night. Zach lives an hour and a half away from Ellensburg. We're finally meeting after three months of texting. I've never been on a date before. I picked a Mediterranean place because he mentioned it on the phone once. I grab a table in the restaurant and wait for him to arrive.

Zach is running late. I send him another message.

> Hey I just got here

> I'm sitting at the table in the back left

Hopefully he'll be here soon. The waitress comes to take my order.

"I'm still waiting on my friend," I say.

But twenty minutes go by. Why hasn't he answered my text yet? I keep glancing out the window, hoping to see him outside. Eventually, the waitress comes back again.

"Sorry, he'll be here soon."

"Alright, sweetie, but we have a long wait tonight."

There's still no reply from him. Hopefully everything is alright. After another twenty minutes pass, I'm forced to give up the table and wait outside. It's starting to rain a little. I'm standing on the sidewalk, trying not to get my hair wet.

Then my phone vibrates. A text from Zach. Finally.

> Sorry. I can't make it anymore

For a second, I think he's joking.

> what do you mean? Is something wrong

> I'm just not ready for this. Should have told you sooner

> but you asked me to come all the way here

> I know, I'm sorry. It just doesn't feel right

I don't know what to say back. We made all these plans together.

> Should we try another day?

The text doesn't go through. At first, I think it's my cellphone signal. Then I check the app and see his profile has vanished. I search for our old messages, but they're all gone. This must have been an accident, right? How am I gonna reach him again? It's raining harder all of a sudden. The next bus home won't come for another few hours. I wasn't expecting to spend this evening alone. I stare at the blank screen. Then I send another text and find a bench to sit on.

I don't know how much time passes. But at some point, someone appears at my side, placing an umbrella over my head. I don't even have to look up to know who it is.

"What are you doing out in the rain?" Sam keeps the umbrella steady as I lift my head. He must have left soccer practice early to come find me.

"Oh, you know . . . just wanted some fresh air."

"In Redmond?"

Maybe I should just tell the truth. After all, he came all the way here. I let out a breath and say, "I was supposed to meet Zach for the first time. But he never showed up."

"Did he know you were coming?"

"We've been planning it for a while." I point toward the restaurant down the street. "I told him I didn't mind taking the bus here. I guess it was a waste of time."

"I'm sorry, Oliver."

I shrug. "It's okay. I mean, it could have been worse, right?"

"Sure, you were too good for him anyway."

"You're my best friend. You have to say that."

"I'm serious," he says. "You deserve better than that, okay? You deserve someone who gives you flowers."

If only that person could be you. Of course, I keep this thought to myself as I rise from the bench and place my head on his shoulder. "Thanks for coming to get me. Let's go home."

"But we're already here," Sam says, smiling. He glances at the restaurant, then back at me. "The place might still be open if you want to go."

"I'm *not* going back in there."

Sam laughs. "Then let's get some pizza."

He puts his arm around me, leading us down the sidewalk. There's a spot right across the street. Sam opens the door, letting me go in first. As I step inside, the memory changes again, pulling me somewhere else . . .

Sunlight fills the café as I come inside. It's the middle of the afternoon and the place is packed. Sam is standing behind the counter, ringing up a customer. It's his first week on the job. I decided to stop by and surprise him at work. Maybe get a free drink while I'm here.

"Excuse me." I cough, making my voice sound deeper. "I'm curious, what's the difference between a latte and a cappuccino? And are the muffins made *fresh*?"

"First of all, they're *scones*," Sam says. "And since when do you drink coffee?"

I hold up a hand. "Now, that's no way to talk to a paying customer," I say, appearing offended. "Can I speak with your manager?"

"Get out."

We both laugh while I lean against the counter. "Alright, Squidward. How's your first week going?"

"Getting the hang of it," he says, tossing a hand towel over his shoulder. "You should have been here during the rush. I had two women screaming at me." He turns around, grabbing something from behind him.

"I hope you're taking advantage of the free drinks."

"I'm actually making one right now—"

Sam sets a steaming cup on the counter. The froth is dusted with sugar.

"Looks fancy," I say.

"It's a honey lavender latte. But it's not for me." For a second, I think it must be for me. Then Sam gestures to a table in the back. "It's for that girl behind you."

"Oh."

"She ordered it the last time she came in. Her name is Julie."

I take a good look at her, trying not to make it obvious. A girl with dull brown hair is sitting at a table alone, writing in her journal. I've never seen her around before.

"I'm kind of nervous to give it to her," Sam says.

"Have you guys talked yet?"

"Not exactly," Sam says. "She's in one of my classes. I think she moved here a few months ago. Do you think I should give it to her? Or would that be weird? Maybe I shouldn't. Unless you think it's a good idea."

At first, I want to tell him no. But it seems like he really wants to. He must really like her, then. I would never want to get in the way of that. "Just go for it. What's the worst that could happen?"

"She could think I'm weird."

"You *are* a little weird," I say. "But maybe she's into that."

"Okay, you're right." Sam takes a deep breath and lets it out. "I'm going to do it." Then he picks up the drink and steps around the counter.

I watch him approach the table and set the cup in front of her. I'm too far away to hear what he's saying, but I figure it's going well when she smiles. At one point, Sam pulls out a chair and sits down next to her. I was hoping he would make a drink for me, too. But I don't want to interrupt their conversation. I give it a moment longer before heading out. He probably forgot I was there anyway.

* * *

The memory changes again. Music pounds through the walls as I come out of the bathroom stall. It's prom of sophomore year. I'm wearing a black button-up, and my hair's slightly wet from the rain. I'm washing my hands when the door swings open and Sam comes in looking for me.

"Oliver! There you are." He smiles wide. "When did you get here?"

"Just a second ago. Had to dry off a little."

I turn off the sink and grab a paper towel. Sam comes around, looking at me in the bathroom mirror. "What's wrong?"

"Nothing."

"Are you sure?"

I try to hide it with a smile. But Sam always knows when something's bothering me. "It's not a big deal," I tell him. "My stepdad was being annoying about his truck again. That's why I had to bike here."

Of course, there's more to the story. I don't feel like talking about it right now.

"You should have told me. I could have picked you up."

I wave it off. "Don't worry about it. My hair looks good wet."

"Glad you made it," he whispers, squeezing my shoulders. "Actually, I want to give you something." There's a white rose pinned to his shirt. I watch as he carefully removes it and pins it on my chest. "There we go."

"You're giving this to me?"

"Thought it might look better on you."

I can't really tell what this means. It's the first flower anyone has ever given me.

"Thanks," I say.

Sam smiles. "Glad you like it. Now let's go back out."

Lights swirl across the gym as we head to the dance floor. Everyone is crowded near the DJ, dancing to The Weeknd. Neither of us came with dates tonight. So when the music slows down, we're both just standing there, nodding along. He looks perfect with his hair brushed to the side. In an alternate world, I would ask him to dance with me. A part of me wonders if he would say yes.

Our friend Sara appears, tapping me on the shoulder. "Hi, Oliver. Would you want to dance?"

"Definitely."

We put our arms around each other, swaying to the music. I glance over and see our other friend Taylor asked Sam to dance, too. They often pair themselves with the two of us, especially for group projects in English class. We dance for a couple songs together. Then Sarah and I decide to head upstairs to get something to drink. When we return to the dance floor, Sam is gone. I ask a few people if they saw where he went.

"*I think he went outside,*" someone says.

"Did he say why?"

But nobody knows the answer to this. Maybe he needed some fresh air. I leave the gym and make my way down the hall. As I push open the door, I find him right away. Sam is in the parking lot, slow dancing with Julie. My heart drops as I stand there, watching them. I didn't even know she was going to be here tonight. He takes her hand as she rests her head against his chest.

I wish I hadn't gone looking for him this time. I touch the rose on my shirt, making sure it's still there as I head back through the door. Everything fades around me, and the memory changes again.

I put on my black domino mask before entering the party. It's Halloween of junior year and the theme is "dynamic duos." Sam and I mulled over a few ideas but ultimately decided on Batman and Robin. I told Sam I didn't mind being Robin. I secretly prefer the golden cape. Plus, I've been told that green is my color.

I find Sam in the kitchen, chatting with Taylor and Sara. They're sitting on the counter, dressed as Velma and Daphne. Sam throws me a can of soda as I approach them.

"*Batman and Robin?*" Taylor says. "Aren't you boys original . . ."

I raise a brow, looking her up and down. "*Velma and Daphne?* At least we're not overshadowed by a *dog*."

"And isn't Daphne's hair red?" Sam asks.

Taylor rolls her eyes, flipping her blond hair over her shoulder. "I'm not dyeing my hair for a party."

"Then you might as well be *Fred*," I say back.

Everyone laughs.

"Where's Julie, by the way?" Sarah asks.

"She's visiting her dad in Seattle," Sam answers.

People are moving toward the living room, where a game of beer pong is being set up. As Sam and I head over to watch, my phone vibrates. There's a long text from my mom. I pause for a second to read it. Unfortunately, there's something going on at home. I had a bad feeling when I left. There's been some issues with my stepdad lately. I was hoping things would get better at some point. I send her a reply, letting her know I'm on the way. Then I turn to Sam. "Do you mind if I borrow your car?"

"What for?" he asks.

"I have to go home for a minute."

"Is something wrong?"

I don't really want to discuss it, but Sam knows enough about the situation to guess for himself. "I just have to go home really quick," I say.

"Okay, I'll go with you."

"You don't have to—"

"No, I'm going with you," he insists.

Sam takes out his keys. Then we head outside and get in the car. I toss my cape in the back seat as he starts the engine. Thankfully, it's not a long drive to my house. I'm nervous as we pull up to the driveway. My stepdad's truck is parked in the garage, meaning he's still at home. I tell Sam to wait in the car, but he follows me anyway.

"Seriously, just stay here."

"I'm going in with you," he keeps saying.

I take a deep breath and open the front door. There's some

clothes lying around, but nothing out of the ordinary. Then I notice a broken dish on the floor.

"Mom? Are you home?"

There's a silence before their bedroom door opens. Mom comes out, carrying a small bag. My stepdad shouts something from inside the room.

"What's going on?" I ask.

Mom shakes her head and whispers, "It's nothing, Oliver." She sets the bag on the table and places her wallet inside.

"Then what is he yelling about?"

"Please ignore him, okay? Just help me get my things."

That's when I understand what's happening. They must have had another fight. I exchange a look with Sam. Part of me is glad he's here now. "Don't worry, we'll help you pack," I say.

I walk her back to the room, where my stepdad is sitting on the bed, watching television. He turns his head toward us, the ceiling fan oscillating above him. I've rarely come into their room while he's here.

"You don't knock?" he sneers.

I don't say anything. Neither does Mom as she crosses the room and retrieves another bag from the closet.

"Where do you think you're going with that?"

She ignores him, grabbing some clothes from the dresser.

"You better answer when I'm talking."

I hate the sound of his voice. And the way he speaks to her. I don't know what the argument was about, but it doesn't matter right now. When he rises from the bed, my stomach tenses. He's not a big guy by any means, so he uses his voice to fill the room.

"Answer me when I ask you a question."

"Don't talk to her like that."

It's the first time I've ever snapped at him.

"Oliver," Mom shushes me.

"You need to watch that boy. And you're not going anywhere." The moment he grabs her bag, something takes over me. I step forward and push him away from her. A lamp falls over as he stumbles to the floor. He looks up at me in shock.

As he rises to his feet, Sam puts himself between us, placing his hands on my shoulders. "Let's help your mom get her things," he says calmly.

But my stepdad isn't nearly as calm. He grabs the lamp and throws it against the mirror, shattering the glass.

My blood boils. I shout at him, "You think I'm scared of you?"

"Why don't you get out!" he shouts.

"Gladly! I never wanted to live here."

"Take your mom with you and don't bother coming back." He turns to her. "You see what you did? Because you keep walking in front of the TV and blocking the game."

That's when it hits me. "Is that what this is about? The stupid television again?" This isn't the first time he's yelled at her for blocking his view or accidentally changing the channel. One time he even threw a plate of food at her. My mom denied it, but I heard it hit the wall from my room.

"You better watch who you're talking to," he says.

"I'm talking to an asshole, that's who."

"Get the hell out of my house!"

Sam stays between us, making sure nothing happens. Eventually, my mom finishes packing and zips up her bags.

"Please, let's go, boys," she says. Sam picks up her bag and walks her to the door.

"I hope you enjoy sleeping on the street," he spits at her.

I clench my first, turning to Sam. "Take my mom to the car," I whisper.

"Oliver . . ."

"*Just do it.*"

Sam presses his lips tight. Then he takes her out of the room. I'll probably regret this later. But the anger I've built up over the last four years breaks like a dam. I grab the golf club he keeps behind the dresser and smash it into the television screen. Then I toss it to the floor. "*There.* Problem solved."

His face burns red as he begins to scream at me. But I quickly leave the room before things get worse. Sam is calling my name from outside. As I walk through the front door, the night air wraps around me and the memory changes one last time . . .

Everything goes dark for a moment. Then pinpricks of light illuminate a night sky as a bonfire comes to life behind me. It's the last night of senior week. I'm standing at the cliffside, staring off at the mountains. As I turn my head, Sam is right there beside me. We look at each other for a moment. The others are drinking and laughing in the background.

"You're oddly quiet tonight," he says.

I shrug. "You know me . . . Just thinking."

"About what?"

"The universe. The meaning of life. How we'll probably never do this again." I place my hands in my pockets, sighing. "You know, since you're leaving me."

"Don't be so dramatic. I'll only be a few hours away."

"You might as well be in another country."

Sam is moving to Portland, Oregon, with Julie for college. They've been dating for almost three years now. I swear it was only yesterday when I saw them talking for the first time. "You know I'll visit all the time," he assures me. "And we still have the whole summer together. We could go on a trip. Just you and me."

"You promise?"

Sam smiles. "Anywhere you want to go."

The thought of this makes me feel better. The two of us traveling somewhere around the world. Things haven't been the same since he started dating Julie. She's spending the week in Seattle, visiting her dad again. I was sort of relieved when he told me she couldn't come tonight. I've been thinking about finally telling him how I feel. I've imagined this moment a thousand times before, but for some reason I still haven't quite figured out the words yet.

Sam glances at the fire for a moment. I'm sure he wants to rejoin the others soon. So I should probably do this now. There's only so much time left before graduation. Who knows if I'll get another chance before then. I take a deep breath and say, "Sam . . . there's something I've been wanting to tell you."

"What is it?"

"I'm not really sure how to say it. Because I don't want to change anything between us . . ." My voice fails.

"Just tell me," he says.

"Alright, what I mean is to say is—"

But Sam's phone goes off. He glances at the screen. "Oh my god."

"What is it?"

"I have ten missed calls from Julie," he gasps. "I was

supposed to pick her up over an hour ago! I think she's walking home all alone now." He tries calling her back, but it goes to voicemail. "She's going to hate me for this. I should go—" He puts his phone away and heads off. Then he spins back to me. "Wait, were you gonna say something?"

The moment is gone now. I just smile at him and say, "Don't worry about it. I'll tell you another time."

"I'm really sorry about this. I'll text you when I get home, okay?"

"You're not coming back?"

Sam frowns. "Probably not. Julie's over an hour away, and I still need to drop her off."

"That really sucks."

"I know. We'll hang out this weekend though. I promise."

As we hug goodbye, I get this strange feeling in my chest. I don't know how to explain it. But it makes me want to hold on to him a little longer. The feeling stays with me as I watch him walk away.

I didn't know that would be the last time I saw him. That there wouldn't be a later for us. That I would wait up all night for a text that was never coming. *That I lost him. And I didn't even know it.*

March 6 at 11:45 PM

It's been almost a year without you

I still can't believe you're gone

CHAPTER ONE

A paper cherry blossom falls from the shelf and lands gently on the carpet. I watch Julie bend down to pick it up. She examines each fold before placing it on her desk. Then she lifts a moving box from the floor and says, "Can you grab the other one, Oliver?"

I fold my arms. "I don't know why you're packing this much."

"Four months is a long time."

"Which is exactly why you shouldn't go."

Julie lets out a breath. "You could at least pretend to be excited for me."

It's our last day together before she heads to Copenhagen. She's doing a study abroad program, abandoning me for the next few months. It's spring quarter of freshman year. Julie and I both attend Central Washington University. Whose door am I going to knock on when I get locked out of my dorm at two in the morning? Who am I going to convince to skip class with me and grab free bagels at the fourth floor of the library?

Julie holds up a candle. "Do you want this?"

"Can't," I groan. "My new roommate says he hates 'feminine' scents." Ethan is your standard straight baseball player with whom I have nothing in common. But he isn't the worst guy in the world.

"I don't know how you're gonna put up with that."

"At least he didn't sleep with my ex," I remind her.

"I thought we agreed not to mention Nolan anymore." She gives me one of her looks. "You better not text him while I'm away."

I return the look. "And what would I even have to say to him after what he did? That I forgive him for cheating on me . . . *with my roommate*?"

Julie sighs. "I thought you were healing from this, Oliver."

I stare out the window. "I'll heal when I'm ready."

Unfortunately, Nolan is also a student at CWU. I met him a few weeks after high school graduation, when he led my group's campus tour. I'd thought it was serendipity when we sat next to each other in the same computer science class I was shopping my first quarter. I ultimately dropped it, but he invited me to my first college party. Long story short, he was my first relationship. We spent every day together. We were practically inseparable. It was a great five months until he started hooking up with Connor, my former roommate. I don't speak to either of them anymore. That's another reason to be sad Julie's leaving. She's one of the few people I have left.

YOU'VE FOUND OLIVER

While Julie's packing up some books, I walk over to her desk and rummage through one of the boxes. I take out a picture frame and hang it back on her wall. Then I grab a stack of books and return them to their spot on the shelf.

Julie turns her head, noticing me. "Oliver, stop that." She takes the books from my hands and places them inside the box again. "I didn't invite you here to unpack my things."

I drop my head. "But I don't want you to go."

"I won't be gone forever. We'll still talk every day."

"It won't be the same though. You're the only friend I have left."

"You're so dramatic," she says, shaking her head. "Everyone loves you. You just need some time to settle in."

As she moves the box away from me, something falls to the floor.

I bend down to pick it up.

It's a guitar pick.

I don't have to ask where she got it. I can hear the strings as his fingers move along them. I turn it in my hands, watching the light bounce off the plastic.

"You can have it, if you'd like," Julie says.

I hadn't noticed her watching. I shake my head and say, "No, that's okay. It's yours." She's given me a lot of Sam's things already. So I hand this one back. I'm sure it means a lot to her.

"Thank you."

We haven't talked about him in a while. I wonder if Julie is thinking the same thing. "You know, it's been almost a year now," I remind her. "Since it happened, I mean." Sam died in the spring of senior year. It took place on the night of the bonfire. As he was driving to find Julie, another car swerved into his lane and crashed straight into him before driving off. I didn't know about it until the next morning, after he'd been found at the side of the road.

"Yeah . . . I know."

"Do you still think about him a lot?"

"Every day."

"Same."

A silence passes. Then she takes my hands and says, "And I know he would want us to live out our lives. I'm sure he would be happy to know we're friends. And me leaving isn't going to change that."

I don't say anything. Even though Julie and I have known each other since sophomore year, we only became friends in the last several months. It's funny how shared grief can bring people together. I know she'll be back at the end of the summer. But then Julie is transferring to Reed College in the fall. She received her acceptance letter a few weeks ago. It was always her plan to move out of Ellensburg. A plan that had once included Sam. "I was thinking about visiting him later," I mention. "Bring him some flowers or something. If you wanted to come with me. We could grab something to eat on the way."

"You know I would love to," she says, squeezing my hand. "But I still have a lot of packing to do. And I should probably spend time with my mom before I go."

I frown. "I'll go alone, then."

"Don't be sad," she says. "Everything's going to be fine, alright? Four months isn't that long, if you think about it. And we'll video call every day."

"Alright, I'll stop guilt-tripping you."

"Good. Because my flight is nonrefundable. Maybe I'll

see you again before I leave?"

"If I can wake up that early."

Julie smiles. Then she checks the time. There's a pile of clothes on the bed that need folding. "I should probably get back to packing."

"You don't need any help?"

"I think you've done enough for today, Oliver."

"Sounds like my cue to leave."

I give her a hug goodbye and see myself out. There's a slight chill as I make my way through town. Usually, I listen to my "sad boy" playlist on these walks alone. But I left my headphones back at the dorm. My new roommate is probably there, blasting country music.

I take out my phone and send a text.

> Julie is moving tomorrow

> What am I supposed to do without the both of you?

It brings me comfort to see his name on the screen. *Sam Obayashi*. Even though he's gone, I still text him sometimes. Maybe more often than I'd like to admit. It makes me feel like we're still connected. Like he's still here. After all, he passed so abruptly and I never got the chance to say goodbye. I didn't plan for the messages to continue this long though. Maybe this is my way of keeping him alive. I like to imagine he's receiving my texts in an alternate universe or something.

* * *

I haven't had much to eat today. My favorite bakery is a few blocks from here. They've been around forever, and they have these almond croissants I always treat myself with after failing an exam. All of my birthday cakes growing up were made there. Sadly, the place is closing down soon. They've been struggling to compete with the chain supermarket that just opened across the street. So I should probably enjoy them while they last.

As I turn the corner, the red-and-yellow-striped canopy comes into view. Maybe I'll also grab something to bring home for Mom. She loves their cardamom buns. But when I try the handle, the door is locked. I press my nose to the window and look inside. All the tables and chairs are gone. There's a sign next to the door.

WE THANK YOU FOR THIRTY YEARS OF BUSINESS

But I thought they were closing next month? I didn't even get to have one last almond croissant. Now I'll have to find somewhere else to go. I turn around and make my way into town. The sign for Sun and Moon blinks across the street. It's the local café where Sam used to work. I've been avoiding it lately for obvious reasons. Even though it's been almost a year, I always think of him when I step through that door.

If I close my eyes, I can see him behind the counter, waiting for me to show up. I used to stay until closing time, blasting music through the speakers while he cleaned up. Thankfully, the place isn't too crowded today. But I'm not planning to stay very long. I just grab a chocolate muffin and head outside again.

"Those are scones," he'd always correct me.

"Tastes like a muffin to me."

I finish it on my way to the flower shop at the corner.

Sometimes, I'll go in to look at all the bouquets they have displayed. But I'm here for a different reason today. I grab some white roses and pay at the counter. They always remind me of the night of our school dance, when Sam pinned his boutonniere onto my shirt.

"*I knew it would look better on you.*"

It's not a long walk to Memorial Hill. I've been enough times by now to know all the shortcuts. The iron posts near the entrance gates stand like giant sentries. I continue past them and make my way up to Sam's grave.

As usual, there are some flowers here already. Someone else must have visited him recently. I have a feeling it was Julie. I kneel down and arrange the stone vase, placing the roses in the middle. I wonder if he would know which ones are from me. *I remember how much you wanted flowers. I'm sad this is the reason you're finally getting them.*

I usually keep him company on nice days like this, sitting in the grass while the clouds roll by. Sometimes, I'll even play music from my phone. We never had the same taste though. He was more of a classic rock guy. Sam and I used to fight over who got to control the speaker. Now I miss the songs he used to play. There's this one that's been stuck in my head. But I can't remember the name.

I send him another message.

> I can't remember the name of that one song you said you liked. It's from that band with the color in their name.

> The violet something?

> Where the guitar goes na naa naaa and the guy's kinda mumbling about his daughter or something like that

This is going to bother me for weeks. I wish I had a made a playlist of all his favorites. So I could listen to them whenever I missed him. When I first started coming here, I would talk to Sam for hours. Update him on everything going on in my life. But it feels like he isn't here anymore. Like no one is listening. That doesn't stop me from visiting him, because I think he would do the same for me.

I stare out at the hill, watching the clouds form overhead. The weather says there's a chance of showers. So I'll have to keep this visit short. Maybe I'll stop by again tomorrow. I hang around for a few more minutes before heading home.

Things are quiet when I return to my dorm. My roommate must be at practice or something. Ethan is on the college baseball team. He and I don't talk very much unless he's asking me where I put his protein powder. But his parents paid for a flex wall to separate our beds and even installed a ceiling curtain for extra privacy. So I can't really complain. Especially when he was probably expecting to live alone this quarter.

Originally, my plan was to live at home the first couple of years. That's what Julie's been doing to save some money. But Mom and I moved to a one-bedroom apartment after she left my stepdad, and the place is too small for the both of us. At least I'm getting the traditional experience of living on campus, even though I'm only a short walk from home.

I sit at the foot of my bed and text Sam again.

> Just got back to my dorm

> the white roses are from me btw

Out of habit, I scroll through all the messages I've sent him. Paragraphs upon paragraphs with no response. I know this can't go on forever, but there's something comforting about it. I've managed to keep this a secret from everyone. I haven't even told Julie about it. I wonder what she would say if she found out. *"It's time to let him go, Oliver. Sam would want that for us."*

Sometimes, it feels like everyone else has moved on with their lives. They even took down the picture of him on our school's website. Meanwhile, his things are everywhere in my room, covering it like handprints. His plaid shirt on the back of my desk chair. The photo of us on the edge of my mirror. Tomorrow will be exactly one year since his accident. I'd promised myself the messages would have stopped by now. That I would finally say goodbye.

But I don't know if I'm ready to give this up yet. After thinking it over, I decide to write to him one last time. Give him a proper goodbye.

> I'm sure you noticed I've been texting you more recently

> Maybe you already guessed why

> It's hard to believe it's been a year since you died. It feels weird to even write it out. I don't think I've said the words out loud yet

> Some days have been harder than others. Writing these texts helps me forget you're gone. But it's starting to feel like I'm talking to myself. That you're not reading them anymore

> You know, Julie keeps telling me you'd want us to move on. I'm sure she's right. In a different universe, I never lost you. Sadly that's not the one I'm living in

> I think about you every second

> But it's time to let you go

> So this will probably be the last message from me

> Goodbye Sam

> Sorry it took me a year to say this

> I'll miss you more than you know

I read over the final message before hitting send.

I should delete his number, too. Otherwise I'll end up texting him again in a moment of weakness. I pull up Sam's contact information. As I press the delete button, a prompt appears on my screen with his name in bold letters.

Are you sure you want to delete **Sam Obayashi***?*

My finger hesitates over the screen. This is somehow harder than I imagined. *Sam is already gone,* I remind myself. *It's only a number on my phone. So just delete it already.*

But I can't seem to press the button. It feels like I'm erasing him from my life. And I can't do that to him. So I hit cancel instead.

That's when I hear something. A ringing coming from the phone. I must have accidently called the number. I should probably end the call. For some reason, I let it continue. Maybe it will go to his voicemail. Should I leave him one last goodbye message?

Suddenly, someone answers the phone.

"Hello?" says a male voice.

Time goes still for a moment. I must have imagined that, right? Because it couldn't be . . .

"Sam?"

CHAPTER TWO

There's a silence before the voice answers.

"No . . . This isn't him."

My heart drops, realizing the mistake. "Sorry, wrong number—"

I hang up immediately. My hands are shaking as I shoot up from the bed. *What's wrong with you? Of course that wasn't Sam.* I should have known his number would have been given to someone else by now. I swear, I'm losing my head. As I'm pacing the room, trying to collect myself, I get a text message notification. It's from Sam's number.

I'm sorry about your friend

I stare at the message, confused. How does he know about Sam? I'm about to freak out when it suddenly hits me. All the messages I've been sending. This stranger must have been reading them the whole time. I can feel my heart pounding in my chest. Those messages were never meant for anyone else to see. I should just block his number, delete the messages, and pretend none of this happened. He probably thinks I'm some crazy person. Maybe I should just explain myself.

> Sorry for all the text messages. I didn't realize someone else had this number

> I won't bother you again

I think that's the end of it. But I get a text back, almost instantly.

Don't worry about it

Sam sounds like he was a great guy

I can't believe how much this stranger knows about me. I'm so embarrassed of this. I shouldn't respond again, but I can't help myself.

> yeah he was

I didn't mean to call you btw. It was an accident

No worries. I was surprised to see your call

> I was surprised someone picked up

> I can imagine lol

This makes me smile a little. At least he has a sense of humor. I send him another text.

> How long have you had this number? If you don't mind me asking

> since last summer

That was over seven months ago. How many texts of mine has he read? It must have been hundreds at this point. I think back to all the things I've said. I've been talking to Sam as if he was still alive. Wishing him happy birthday. Telling him how much I miss him. All the words I never got to say in person.

> god that's so embarrassing

> I can't believe I've been texting you this whole time

> Don't be embarrassed

> I get it

> Thanks for being so understanding. And sorry for the way I hung up too

> You sort of sounded like him tbh

> oh really?

Maybe I shouldn't have said that.

> Just a little bit. It's been a minute since I heard his voice

> How old was he? If that's okay to ask

> he would have turned nineteen this year

> We're the same age then

He must be a freshman, too.

> Where are you from?

> I go to school in Seattle. But I'm from Bellevue

> wbu?

Bellevue is about an hour away from here. At first, I think that's too many coincidences. Then I remember we share the same area code, so it makes sense that he would live nearby.

> I'm in Ellensburg

> Central Washington university?

> Yup. The Harvard of the Pacific Northwest

> Is that right?

> You know what they say, if you can make it here, you can make it anywhere

> Thought that was nyc

> New York is overrated

> Agreed

This is such a surreal conversation, seeing Sam's name pop up on my phone again. Of course, I know it's not him. I sit back on the bed, watching the three dots move as he's typing. To my surprise, we talk for a while. He goes to the University of Washington, which is admittedly the better school. We ask each other about the different classes we're taking. How the quarter is going so far. He's majoring in astronomy, and possibly minoring in math, making me question my work ethic. I want to get to know him more. But eventually, he has to head off to dinner with some friends.

> Have to go soon. It was nice to finally talk though

> Yeah same

I should probably leave it there. But I want to say one more thing.

> Thanks for picking up the phone btw

YOU'VE FOUND OLIVER

He takes a few minutes to respond. Then the text notification chimes again.

> I'm glad you called

> I know I already said this. But I'm sorry about your loss

> I can tell you really cared about him

For a second, I forgot that he knows about Sam. About me, too. Yet I know so little of him.

> I appreciate that. Have a great night

> You too

The conversation ends. I lie in bed thinking about him for the rest of the night. I can't help but read over our messages. I wonder if we'll ever talk again. Every time I texted Sam's number, I always imagined getting a response one day. But I never expected it to be from someone else.

CHAPTER THREE

I wake up late the next morning, which has become part of my routine. It's the start of a new quarter, and I still need to figure out my schedule. There are a few courses I plan to shop this week. I'm hoping to get into one of those big lectures where I can sleep in the back row without anyone noticing.

Ethan is awake when I pull back my curtain. I can hear him through our flex wall, playing video games with music on in the background. There's protein powder spilled all over the desk we use as a dining table. At least his boxers aren't tossed on the floor again. But there are plastic bottles everywhere. I resist the urge to be his maid and clean up after him. So I leave it all there as I grab my phone and head to the bathroom.

There are a few messages from Julie. Copenhagen is nine

hours ahead, making it difficult for us to talk on the phone. But it's nice to wake up knowing there will be a text from her. Like she's writing to me from the future.

> Just stepped off the plane. Didn't sleep a wink so I'm exhausted

> Have a great first week!

> Please don't do anything you'll regret

What's that supposed to mean? If she thinks I can't survive without her, then she shouldn't have left. Admittedly, she has talked me out of a few bad decisions. Like purchasing an essay from a random website online. Or texting Nolan back when he wanted to talk things through. It's going to be a tough few months without her here. I send her a response before heading to the shower.

> I make no promises

> How are the boys there?

> Send me videos of your room already

It's peak cherry blossom season. Petals are falling from the trees as I cut through the quad. I'm walking a little faster than usual. The psychology class I'm shopping starts in a few minutes, and I don't want to be late on the first day.

I've never been in the psychology building before. The lecture hall is massive, lined with ten rows of seats that are filling up fast. I manage to find a spot in the middle as the professor writes something on the chalkboard. I don't have the textbook yet, so I'm just listening as he goes over the syllabus for the course.

I'm not really paying attention though. I keep glancing at my phone, reading the conversation from last night. I still can't believe someone else has Sam's number. And I don't even know his name. For some reason, I can't stop thinking about him. I wonder what he looks like. Part of me wants to send him another text. Ask him how his day is going or something. But that would be weird, right? I mean, we don't even know each other. And it's not like we're friends or something. I should probably just forget about it.

The class ends a few minutes over. People are packing up while the professor erases the board. I can't believe there's already an assignment for next week. I'm not sure if I'm going to stay in the course. But I jot down the pages just in case.

There are a few hours to kill before my next class. Usually, I would meet up with Julie at the library around this time. But I don't feel like going there alone right now. So I take a stroll through the quad and enjoy the fresh air. Maybe I'll pick up a sandwich at the to-go bar.

As I turn the corner, my body freezes.

His blond hair always sticks out from the crowd. Nolan stands near the history building, staring down at his phone. I would recognize that suede jacket from a mile away. He wears it everywhere, thinking it brings out the blue in his eyes. I should probably turn around before he notices me.

But I watch him for a moment, curious if he's waiting for someone. Like the way he used to always wait for me.

For a second, I think about saying hi. Would that really be so bad? Maybe we could be friends at some point. Truth is, I'm sad about the way things ended. Despite what happened, I miss hanging with him. It's been almost two months since we broke up. He's reached out a few times, asking if we can "chat." Maybe I'm just feeling extra lonely since Julie left, but I miss having someone to see every day. Julie would be disappointed if she knew I talked to him. I would be disappointed in myself, too.

"After what he's done, you don't owe him anything," she would say.

A church bell goes off in the background, bringing me back to my senses. I head off before I do something I'll regret later.

Everyone's out on the grass this afternoon. Usually, I would look for a spot in the shade to lie down and relax. Instead, I head to the dining hall to grab a sandwich. There's an empty bench outside by the gardens. To be honest, I haven't had much of an appetite these past few weeks. But I force myself to take a few bites of this turkey sandwich anyway. I wonder how Julie's first day went. I think about giving her a call, but she's probably getting ready for bed.

Maybe I'll head back to my dorm. Hopefully, Ethan has left by now. I finish the sandwich and throw the wrapper away. As I'm walking back, my phone goes off.

There's a new message from Sam's number. I open it instantly.

Lady Godiva's Operation

What the heck does that mean? He must have sent it to me by mistake. I respond with a single question mark and wait for his response.

> It's the name of the song

> The one you were asking about

At first, I don't know what he's talking about. Then I remember the message I sent yesterday afternoon. About that song that's been stuck in my head. The one I forgot the name of. "Lady Godiva's Operation." That's what it was called!

omg you're right

That's the song!

> Was debating if I should tell you

> Wasn't sure if it would be weird

It's not weird at all

You should have told me sooner. It was torturing me

> I had to think about it for a second. Looked up bands with the word violet. Then I realized you meant velvet. It's by the Velvet Underground

The Velvet Underground. No wonder I couldn't find it.

> Yes!! Can't believe I forgot their name

> To be fair, they haven't been around in a while

I smile at this. We're texting each other again. It's a little strange seeing Sam's name pop up instead. I want the conversation to continue. So I think of something else to say.

> How are your classes going?

> I'm actually sitting in one right now. But the professor's running late

> So I'm distracting myself

> Happy to be your distraction

He hearts the message.

> Are you listening to the song? It's stuck in my head now

> About to blast it in my dorm

He sends me a link to some video.

> Found this live version online earlier. It's from their concert in Paris circa 1968

Of course, I heart the video.

> Ooo saving this for later. Need the full screen experience

> It's a little grainy. Given it was recorded almost 60 years ago

A second later, he follows up with another text.

> Professor just walked in.

> Text you later

I stare at his message. *Text you later.* Does that mean he wants to keep talking to me? I see myself reflected in the screen, smiling. I can't believe he actually texted me first. And I still don't even know his name. I'll remember to ask him for it next time. I linger for a moment, taking this all in. Then I put my earbuds in and look up the song. "Lady Godiva's Operation" by the Velvet Underground.

The second the guitar comes in, a memory of Sam plays in my head. I always forced him to change the song when this one came on. But now I listen to it on repeat for the next few hours.

✷ ✷ ✷

I head home for dinner that evening. The television is on when I come inside. Mom is cooking in the kitchen. I can smell garlic bread in the toaster oven. Since I live close to home, I try to stop by as often as I can. But schoolwork can sometimes keep me away. That's why we came up with Thursday night dinners. It's the only day of the week she takes off. Mom works as a waitress at this Greek restaurant outside of town. It was the first job she could get after we moved out of my stepdad's place.

"Knock, knock," I say.

Our kitchen is a little cluttered. Looks like we're having chicken again. Mom kisses me on the forehead and says, "We're out of olive oil."

"I could have picked it up on the way."

"No, it's fine. I'll get some from work tomorrow."

I grab some plates from the cabinet and help set the table. I always bring out Mom's favorite ceramic dish. It's the one we made together at a pottery class on her birthday. It also happened to be the night Nolan hooked up with Connor. But I try not to let that taint the memory. I know how much the gift meant to Mom. She painted it seafoam green, which she says is the color of my eyes. There's a photo of us from that night on the refrigerator.

Mom scoops the potatoes onto my plate. "How was school?"

"Not too bad. Still figuring out my schedule."

"I hope you're getting along with your new roommate."

"Ethan? He's alright, I guess." I take a bite of the chicken. "I mean, he's no prince charming, but he could worse."

"As in the prince of Wales?" She shakes her head. "You must not be watching the news. Nothing royal about that family."

I tell her about the classes I'm shopping. There's a couple more I'm checking out this week. Mom asks if Julie made it safe to Copenhagen. I let her know she texted me the second she got off the plane. I'm planning to wake up early to call her in the morning.

"Did you visit Sam today?"

I don't answer this right away. Mom knows how hard this year has been. After all, she watched us grow up together. He came over to our house a thousand times. She would make snacks for us when we played video games in the living room. So I know she misses him, too. . . .

"No, but I did yesterday."

Mom nods. "I'm sure he appreciates that." She doesn't ask me any more questions about it. But he's all I think about as I finish the rest of my plate.

After dinner, we put on a television show in the living room. Mom is a big fan of period dramas. It's nice to sit down with her and make fun of the costumes. But I can only stay for one episode tonight. There's some reading I need to get done before bed. As usual, Mom wraps up food for me to take back. She kisses me on the cheek and stands by the front door until I'm out of sight.

It's always nice to visit home. I know how much Mom appreciates spending time together. She always says I'm the only man left in her life.

* * *

It's 9:05 when I get back to my dorm. The lights are off, which means Ethan is probably out with friends again. I head to my side of the room and close the curtain. Then I fall face-first into bed and rest my eyes for a few minutes. Hopefully, Ethan doesn't bring a girl back tonight. I have to get up for a 9:00 AM class. I probably wouldn't bother if I didn't think the professor was cute—at least by forty-year-old-bald-guy standards. Thankfully, it's only once a week.

I turn on my side, checking my phone again. I was hoping to get another text from him. The guy with Sam's phone number. Maybe I should change the contact name to something else, since it doesn't belong to Sam anymore. I wish I knew his name so I could look him up. I want to know everything about him. What color is his hair? Does he have siblings? A dog? My finger hovers over the keyboard as I think of something to write.

I know I should wait until tomorrow. But I can't help myself.

I send him another message.

> How was the rest of your day?

God, I'm so bad at this. I should have said something more interesting. Like mention the song we've been talking about. Twenty long minutes go by with no response, making me regret my decision. I bet he deleted my number already. I'll probably never hear from him again.

Then my phone goes off. There's a new message.

> Hey

> I was just thinking about you

I exhale with relief and push myself up. He was thinking about me. What should I say back?

> Was thinking about you too
>
> Glad to know you're not sick of me

of course not haha

Wasn't expecting to hear from you though

It's a nice surprise

> Sorry, I'm just used to texting this number
>
> Hard to break a habit you know?

To be honest, I've gotten used to seeing your number pop up, too

Always wondered if it would stop one day

I think about the messages I sent before. How vulnerable they all were.

> I'm still embarrassed about that . . .

> I never thought anyone was reading those messages

You shouldn't be

Sam was very lucky to have you as a friend

I smile at this.

> That really means a lot

> What's your name by the way?

Ben

You?

> Oliver

Nice to finally put a name to this number

> Same

Did you watch the video?

They also do Sweet Jane too.
Was listening to it a second ago

> Gonna add it to my playlist right now

But let me know what you think

> Have to finish up this assignment before midnight

> I will

> glad we got to chat again

> I am too

> It's nice to know who's on the other side

The conversation ends. But now we know each other's names. I'm smiling as I lie back down. I should really get some work done, too. At least read a couple chapters or something. Instead, I play the video he sent and let the music fill the room.

"*Ben.*"

I whisper his name to myself. The boy with Sam's phone number. I read over the messages again.

It's nice to know who's on the other side.

CHAPTER FOUR

James E. Brooks Library is a labyrinth of liminal space. I spent the morning wandering the second floor, collecting books left out on the endless shelves. One wrong turn could send me straight to The Backrooms. I've been working here for a few weeks. It's part of a federal work-study program for students with financial needs. It's honestly a nice gig so far.

Once the cart is full, I roll it back to the circulation desk. Rami is checking out someone's book as I take the seat next to him. He's a first-year like I am. I see he's still working on his little project. Someone dropped a copy of *Swann's Way* in a bathtub, damaging most of the pages. I told Rami we should just put in an order for a new one, but he brought in a flat iron to straighten out every page.

"It's starting to look like new," I say.

"Don't lie to me," he groans, lowering his straightener.

"I've spent six hours on this and I'm not even halfway done."

"You know they don't pay us extra for that, right?"

Rami sighs. "I'm trying to get a raise, okay?"

"I don't think the pay is negotiable."

"Then what am I burning my fingers for?" Rami tosses the book into the recycling and crosses his arms. I let him take a break while I help the next person in line.

I spend the next hour sorting through a cart full of go-backs, pausing to check my phone every few minutes. I texted Ben this morning, letting him know I watched the Velvet Underground concert last night. To be honest, it almost put me to sleep. I wasn't a fan of the band when Sam was alive, and I wouldn't say I am now. But I wanted something to text Ben about.

I'm sure Ben will respond eventually. He's probably just in class right now. I read over our previous messages in the meantime.

"What are you smiling about?"

I look up from my phone. Rami is sipping an iced coffee, a brow raised at me.

"Nothing," I say.

"It's not Nolan, is it? Because you're not supposed to be talking to him."

"How do you know about . . ." I pause. Because the answer is obvious. "Is Julie having you keep tabs on me?"

Rami shrugs. "Maybe, maybe not."

I had a feeling she asked some of our friends to watch over me, but I can't believe she would take it this far. Rami and I only see each other at work. I don't need him keeping track of my every move. How many other people does she have spying on me?

"Well, stop that. You don't work for her, okay?"

"Yeah, but she kind of scares me."

I let out a breath. Frankly, Julie scares a lot of people. Some might even describe her as unlikable at times. I mean, it took her a few years to show me her softer side. But now she's my best friend in the world. "She only pretends to bite," I say.

"I'm not taking any chances. She has quite the . . . *reputation* in the English department." He takes another sip of coffee and turns back to his keyboard.

Honestly, you've got to respect her for leaving an impression. And at least I know she's doing this out of love. I turn my chair around, checking my phone again. Still no response from Ben. But there's a text from someone else. Speak of the devil herself.

> Hey. Are you still taking my mom's seminar?

> Yeah I was planning to

> Isn't it right now?

I glance at the time. The class started ten minutes ago.

> shittt

> Oh Oliver . . .

I should have planned my work schedule better. I tell Rami to cover for me for the next two hours. Then I grab my bag and sprint out the doors.

Julie's mom is a professor in the philosophy department. The course is called Disrupting the Senses. For some reason, it's cross-listed in psychology, film and media studies, religious studies, and also German. Apparently, she has a reputation of being a little out there. I'm hopeful she'll be lenient on the grading. I mean, I have dinner at their house all the time. I've even helped with the dishes before. I'm sure that should give me some favoritism.

Thankfully, the building isn't too far. I hurry up the stairs and open the classroom door. Julie's mom is in the middle of answering a question when I walk in slowly. ". . . yes, of course, but I would like us to think beyond that. Now, what are some other things we can *sense*? For instance, when something is missing. Or wrong. *Colors?* What about when something changes in the air? Or a person's mood?"

Quietly, I find a seat in the back. As I pull out the chair, Professor Clarke turns her head and says, "Oliver! What are you doing all the way back there? There is an open spot here in the front."

I wasn't expecting her to call me out. I grab my bag and make my way down. Everyone watches as I take a seat right in the front.

"Glad you could join us today," she says, gesturing to the rest of the class. "We were just talking about the name of the course. Disrupting the Senses." She pauses, allowing us to take it in. Then she looks at me. "What do you think that means, Oliver?"

"Oh . . . uh." Julie only mentioned this class a few days ago. I haven't even seen the syllabus yet. So I have no clue what it's actually about. "Something to do with our senses?"

She nods. "Yes, what about them?"

"I don't really know."

"That's why we're here, to ask questions," she says, bringing her hands together. Then she turns to someone else. "You in the gray shirt. Looks like you have something to say."

He seems surprised to be called on but manages to answer anyway. "Maybe it has to do with our perception. As in, how we see the world."

"*How we see the world,*" she says, nodding thoughtfully. "Interesting. Would anyone like to expand on that? What are other ways to perceive the world that we haven't discussed yet?" Professor Clarke walks between the rows of seats as she continues. "What about our sense of time? Or the future? What about our *memories*? Do they also shape our image of the world? If so, what exactly does that even mean?"

She gives us a moment, but no one raises their hand. She lets out a slow breath, returning to the front of the class. "It seems a lot of you are afraid to share your thoughts. I want to make something very clear to all of you. There are no wrong answers in this course, which means there is no rubric to follow and no points to deduct. Everyone gets the same grade, as long as you turn in your work. All I ask is you forget what you've learned from your other classes. This is my permission for you to be creative, question everything you've been told, think outside of the box. Speaking of which—"

There's a white box on the table in front of the class. Mrs. Clarke walks over and places her hands on top of it. "This brings us to our first activity. For the remainder of the class, we are going to shift our attention to what's inside of this box in front of us. You're going to guess on your own and then break into small groups to discuss it."

The girl behind me raises her hand. "Are we allowed to

touch it?"

Professor Clarke shakes her head. "The rules are you can't touch it or shake it. And the box will remain closed for the entire class," she says.

A guy in the back raises his hand. "Is this like Schrödinger's cat? Where it's both dead and alive until we open it?"

"*Forget Schrödinger*," she scoffs. "There could be three cats in here. Or even a hundred."

"But there can't be a hundred," he says.

"And who said that?"

"I mean, it's physically impossible."

"*Interesting.*" She looks at the rest of us as if expecting someone to interject. "It seems you all have come to this class with your own *constraints* and *logic* about the world. Not to say any of it is wrong. But for the sake of these ninety minutes we have together, I would like us to open our minds toward what we consider to be impossible." She lets that sink in. Then she grabs a piece of chalk and faces the board.

"Let's take a second to discuss the book we'll be reading this quarter. It's called *The Poetics of Space* by Gaston Bachelard," she says, writing down the title for us. "But I don't want you to read it like any other book. I want you to read it in any order, starting at any page. Just pick a passage and write about it. In fact, it is Bachelard who says there are more things in a closed box than in an open one. We will consider what that means as we continue our activity."

For the next fifteen minutes, she has us write down what we think is inside the box. I guessed a sandwich because that's what I had for lunch. Then we arrange the desks into small circles to "see each other better." As we come up with question for clues, it never feels like we're getting closer to the answer.

Mrs. Clarke doesn't confirm or dismiss anything, making it even more confusing. For a second, I think she might not know what's in there herself.

The class ends a few minutes early. I stick around as everyone files out.

Professor Clarke unzips the bag on her desk. "Nice having you in my class today, Oliver."

"Sorry I was late."

She waves it off. "That's alright. Julie might have given me a warning. I just hope today's conversation didn't scare you off."

"Not at all. It was pretty interesting, actually. I'm definitely planning to come back."

"It wouldn't offend me if you didn't."

I smile. "It was a great lecture. I promise."

"I'm glad to hear that. Now, what else are you taking?"

"I don't know. I'm still shopping around."

"Have you thought about what major you want?"

I let out a breath. "I honestly have no clue. I know Julie decided already." She's practically had her life planned out since sophomore year of high school. Meanwhile, I don't even know what's for breakfast tomorrow.

"We all have our own timelines, Oliver."

"Yeah, I know."

"If anything," she says, "maybe this class will help you figure it out."

"I hope so."

As Professor Clarke packs up her things, I glance at the box on the table. "So what's actually in there, by the way?"

"You know I can't tell you that," she answers.

"My guess is there's nothing inside."

She looks at me, almost surprised. "If that's what you choose to believe, then maybe it's a good thing you're taking this class. Because for all you know, there's an entire universe in there."

I check my phone the second I get out of class. Why hasn't Ben messaged me back yet? It's been a few hours already. I know it shouldn't bother me this much. I mean, we don't even know each other. But I can't seem to get him out of my head. Hopefully, I'll hear from him soon.

I forgot my key card in my room this morning. So I have to wait for someone to let me into the dorm building. There's different music playing in each hallway, like different radio stations. I'm about to try our door handle when I notice the rubber band. From what I learned in movies, that's the universal roommate code for "do not disturb." We never discussed it before though. Maybe I'll just knock first.

A moment later, Ethan cracks open the door. But he doesn't let me in. "Hey, what's up?"

"Oh, you know, enjoying the hallway. Are you—"

"Busy, yeah." He points at the rubber band on the knob. "You mind coming back later?"

"What time later?"

Ethan checks his watch. "How about six?"

"*Six?*" I consider this. "Alright. Fine."

"Great. Owe you one—" He shuts the door between us.

That's the longest conversation we've had all week. I should have just asked him to grab my key card. But I don't want to knock again. So I head back down the hallway.

Maybe I'll take a stroll through town.

Someone is waiting outside for me.

"Hey," Nolan says casually.

I nearly trip on the step. I want to turn around, but the door has already closed behind me. I'm waiting for him to head off, but he just stands there with his hands in his pockets.

"What are you doing here?" I finally ask.

"I wanted to see you."

I don't respond.

"And to talk," he admits. "I tried texting you, but I don't think they're going through. Unless you blocked me or . . ."

"How did you know where I moved?"

"Rachel told me."

I should have figured that already. She's one of his best friends, and her younger brother lives on the floor above me.

"So you came here to stalk me . . ."

"I came because I missed you." His voice is softer than usual. "I'm sorry. It was a mistake, okay? I don't want things to end over this." He looks at me with those piecing blue eyes, which might have worked a few months ago.

"I have to go," I say. I try to walk around him. But he puts out a hand.

"Wait, alright? Just tell me what I should do."

"*Nothing.*"

"Can't we at least talk about it?"

"There's nothing to talk about."

Nolan groans. "You're killing me right now. I told you, I'm sorry. I wish it never happened, alright?"

"I wish it didn't, either," I say.

"Oliver—"

I hurry off before he can say more. Thankfully, he doesn't follow after me. I can't believe he was just waiting outside like that. I figured we would run into each other eventually. But I thought it would be at a party or something. I'm not even sure how to feel right now. Because a part of me still misses him. After all, we were together for five months. We spent every day together. I'd never been that close with anyone else. He was the first person I loved since Sam.

A part of me wants to forgive him, pretend like none of this ever happened. Wouldn't life be so much easier that way? As I cut through the school rose garden, I remember what Sam once said. *"You deserve someone who gives you flowers."*

If only you were still here.

I wish I could call Julie and tell her what happened. But it's probably two A.M. in Copenhagen. Maybe I should have gone with her. Moved to a completely different country. At least I know Nolan wouldn't be there. What if I just call her anyway? I mean, she basically manifested this encounter. And this is basically an emergency. As I pull out my phone, there's a text message.

> Hey. Sorry for the late reply

> Was caught up in lab all day. But just got home

> What are you up to?

For a second, I thought he had forgotten about me. I want to reply immediately, but I don't want to seem desperate. Maybe I'll find somewhere to sit down before I answer.

I cross the street and head into town. Sun and Moon doesn't look too packed today. The Moroccan lamps never give the place enough light. I order a pastry and find a table in the corner. Then I glance at my phone again. It's been twenty-three minutes since Ben texted me. Honestly, that's long enough.

> No worries!
>
> finished my last class for the week
>
> my roommate kicked me out of our room
>
> so I'm seeking shelter until I'm allowed back

I'm not expecting a quick reply. But he answers within seconds.

Oh that's brutal

> You're telling me
>
> There goes my afternoon nap

Currently in bed right now

But no time for a nap either.
Have to get back to lab soon

Just enjoying a few minutes of freedom

> You're not really selling this major

There are better days than others. I messed up my experiment earlier and have to redo the whole thing. Also forgot my journal with all my notes

Sorry, I don't usually complain this much

> Don't worry. I'm sure my day was worse

Did you also contaminate your cell culture?

> No but close

Feel free to elaborate

> Don't want to bore you with my lore

I promise you won't bore me

I always enjoy your texts

I probably shouldn't tell him about Nolan. But maybe it's not that big of a deal. I mean, he knows so much about me already, right?

> Just ran into my crazy ex. That's all

Oh

You have my attention

> It's not a big deal. Just haven't seen him in a while

Sounds like you're not on speaking terms

> It's honestly for the best

I get that

I ended things with someone recently too

> Sorry to hear

It's alright. We were only together a few weeks

So I wouldn't really consider him an "ex"

So he was dating another guy. That means he's gay, too.

How long were you guys together?

> Five months

Can I ask why you broke up?

> It's a long story

> Maybe I'll tell you another time

building the suspense I see

> It's not a very good ending. I can tell you that much

> But enough about my love life.
> Tell me more about this cell culture

> You mean the mold I'm growing?
> Riveting stuff really

I smile at the change of subject. We continue texting back and forth. Ben tells me he lives in his own apartment off campus. It's unusual for first years, but he managed to finesse things with the housing office. He asks what my plans are for the rest of the week. There's always a few parties happening in the dorm. But I haven't decided if I'm going yet.

> If I stop responding, it just means I fell asleep

> Don't you have to get back to lab?

> Yeah but my eyes won't stay open

> You should take a nap if you're that tired

> Maybe you're right

> Could you text me in an hour if I don't wake up?

> Setting my alarm now

I smile at our conversation. Ben doesn't respond after that, which makes me think he did fall asleep. I'll remember to check in on him in an hour. Then I finish my drink and head out of the café.

CHAPTER FIVE

Ben and I have been texting each other more and more lately. Between classes, during lunch, even at the library when I should be studying. It's nice having someone to talk with throughout the day. We have each other's schedules memorized now. Ben is taking four classes, five days a week, with Astronomy Club every Wednesday. I don't know how he finds the time to respond to me with his workload. Even on exam nights, we'll fall asleep texting each other.

I asked if we could follow each other on Instagram. But Ben isn't on any social media platforms, except Twitter, which he hasn't used in years. You can barely see him in the profile picture—he's standing far away from the camera, facing the ocean. Thankfully, I found a better picture of him online. It's from a school news article, announcing a scholarship he was awarded senior year. He doesn't look like someone you would find in a lab. He has soft brown eyes, with a sharp jawline, and his dark hair reminds me a little of Sam's. He has the shoulders of a varsity tennis player, which is confirmed in the article I'm reading.

Benjamin Han.

So that's your full name.

Of course, I save the photo on my phone. I wonder if he's looked me up, too. Sadly, there are no articles about me winning any awards. But there is an old Tumblr I made in middle school that's dedicated to Dean Winchester from the show *Supernatural*. I should probably delete that before Ben, or anyone else, finds it.

In other news, Julie seems to be having the best time in Copenhagen. She's been sending me photos of her daily life, which includes the food she's eating. I wish I had the money to visit her while she's studying there.

> And how are things in Ellensburg?

> Any interesting updates for me?

I haven't told her about Ben yet. She'll ask questions that I'm too embarrassed to answer. *So, I've been secretly texting Sam's old number for a year. When I accidently called it, this guy picked up instead. And now I can't stop thinking about him . . . Funny story, right?*

Knowing Julie, she would set up some kind of intervention. So I'll probably keep it to myself for now. Especially since Ben and I haven't even met in person. But I tell her about the Nolan incident.

> What a narcissist

> I can't believe he just showed up like that!

> I'm proud of you for walking away

I don't mention that I still feel guilty about the situation. I mean, he only wanted a few minutes to talk with me. We haven't run into each other since that interaction. A part of me wonders what he would have said. Hopefully, this feeling will eventually go away.

The next morning, I wake up to Ethan's alarm. It's been ringing for ten minutes straight. I swear, that boy can sleep through an earthquake. He'll set five alarms in a row and still somehow end up missing class. Usually, I just put on headphones and try to go back to sleep. But I remember he has some important presentation today, so I decide to wake him up myself. I pull back his curtain and throw a pillow at him. Then I head to the bathroom to take a shower.

It's another gorgeous day on campus. Lacrosse players are practicing in the quad and the tulips are budding along the gardened paths. I'm heading to the library for my Thursday shift. According to Rami, there's free breakfast today. I grab a donut and meet him at the circulation desk. He's sitting at the counter, drinking his usual iced coffee.

"Morning, Rami." I drop my things on the floor and pull out the chair beside him. "Your hair's particularly shiny today. New serum?"

"*Horse shampoo*," he whispers. "I saw a video about it online. Apparently, it's good for the skin, too."

"No wonder you're *glowing*." I glance at his computer screen. "What are you working on?"

"My transfer application."

"Transfer application? Don't tell me you're abandoning me, too."

"I want to go to NYU," Rami says, taking another sip of coffee. "You know, have my Blair Waldorf experience."

"You can get the same experience here. The sororities are full of pretentious rich white girls. And plenty of guys who will cheat on you, too," I add.

"Sure, but the vibes aren't the same."

"You're not leaving me here, okay?"

Someone approaches the counter. "Hey, Oliver."

It's Sarah, another one of Nolan's close friends. I'm bound to run into some of them working here. Admittedly, she was one of my favorites. Her parents own the car dealership in town. We once stayed at their beach house for a weekend.

"Oh. Hi, Sarah."

She smiles. "Haven't seen much of you lately."

"You know"—I shrug—"busy with school."

"I figured." There's a silence as she stands there. Then Sarah lets out a breath and says, "Listen, Oliver. I heard about what happened. I hope you're doing alright."

"I'm doing fine."

"I'm glad to hear that." She finally hands me her book to check out. It's the second edition of *Networks: An Economics Approach*. She and Nolan both major in business administration. They're probably taking this class together. "By the way," she says, "Kat and I are having some people over tomorrow. You should stop by, if you're not busy."

I lie. "Thanks, but I have plans already."

"Got it. Guess I'll see you around." Then she grabs her book and walks off.

Rami leans toward me. "Who was that?"

"One of Nolan's friends."

"And she invited you to hang out? Sounds like a setup."

"You think so?" I consider this for a moment. "I don't know, she's always been nice to me. We used to hang in her room all the time. I'm sure it wouldn't be that big of a deal if I stopped by—"

"I'm telling Julie."

"For just *thinking* about it?"

Rami smacks my arm. "You know Nolan might be there."

"*Fine*. Then I won't go, okay? No need to bring Julie into this."

He's probably right about that. Of course Nolan would be there. That's another thing I miss about dating him. Things were never boring with him. We always had fun weekend plans together. He introduced me to everyone he knew. Now I have to start over and find my own things to do. Even Rami has plans to go bowling with his chess club. I asked if I could tag along, but he says it's pretty exclusive. *Chess members only*. Looks like it's another solo movie night in bed.

After work, I hang in the library and start on my assignments. I have a few chapters to read for American History. I'm supposed to be taking notes, but the textbook is putting me into a coma. The only thing keeping me awake are texts from Ben. He finished his lab early today. Now he's packing to go home to Bellevue for the weekend.

> How long are you going home for?

Staying until Sunday

That's the thing about living close to home. Parents expect me to visit all the time

> No need to tell me. My mom practically lives down the street

> We do Thursday night dinners. I'm not allowed to miss it

That's honestly sweet

What are your plans for the weekend?

> Still figuring them out

Should we meet up?

The question catches me by surprise. I'm not sure if he's serious. We've only been talking for a few weeks.

> As in this weekend?

Yeah

Bellevue isn't too far from you right? We could meet somewhere in the middle

> If you're not busy

I can't believe he actually wants to see me. I was hoping we would meet eventually. But I wasn't expecting it to be this soon.

> That could be fun

> Where should we meet?

> Have you been to North Bend?

> I think it's halfway between us. I actually know a great diner there. Best smash burgers in Washington

I look it up on my phone. It's about an hour drive from Ellensburg.

> That's not too far

> And love a smash burger. But I'll have to judge that for myself

> What about tomorrow?

This is happening so fast. I only have Professor Clarke's class in the afternoon. I could hop on the bus afterwards. Ben texts me the name of the diner. I can't believe we're actually going to meet in person. The thought sends butterflies to my stomach. It's impossible to focus on anything else. But

I force myself to finish the rest of the chapter before leaving the library.

I drop my things off at the dorm before heading home for dinner. We're having turkey meatloaf tonight. I help Mom bring in the groceries and start on the vegetables. I overcook the broccoli a little, but it's still good. Mom saved some galaktoboureko from her shift at the restaurant yesterday. It's this Greek dessert that's made of custard and baked in filo dough. We put on another episode of her period drama and eat in the living room. As usual, she wraps up the leftovers for me to take back.

I can barely fall asleep that night, but morning comes before I know it. I shave my face thoroughly and spend some extra time on my hair.

I can barely pay attention in Professor Clarke's class. She has us do another activity around *The Poetics of Space*. The quote on the board reads, *"We are never real historians, but always near poets, and our emotion is perhaps nothing but an expression of a poetry that was lost."* —Gaston Bachelard. We spend the class drawing our interpretations of it with colored pencils. Professor Clarke walks the room and says, "When we think of a space, we think of our experiences in it. The rooms we walk though, the lives we live there. Are those memories not woven into the walls themselves? What happens to them after we leave?"

For some reason, this makes me think of the lake. The one Sam and I used to escape to all the time. I still find him there in some of my dreams. I remember the picture Sam drew of me, lying out in the grass, surrounded by flowers. For our activity, I try to recreate it with him instead.

The moment class ends, I race out the door, heading

straight to the bus station. Ben sends a text to confirm the location. His parents are letting him borrow their car. I send him an ETA as soon as I step on the bus.

> Text me when you're close

> I'll see you soon

It's an hour-and-a-half journey to North Bend. I take in the views of evergreen trees along the road. I'm a little nervous about meeting him. I steamed my favorite white T-shirt and threw on a jacket. I thought about going with a navy button-up, but I didn't want to be overdressed.

I'm listening to the Velvet Underground album on the way there. Ben seems like a really big fan of them. It's funny that he has that in common with Sam. He still sends me videos of some of their performances every now and then. I should probably be more familiar with their music, but I can only get through a few songs before switching to my pop playlist.

Eventually, the pale gray buildings of North Bend come into view. Somehow, this town seems even smaller than Ellensburg. The bus drops me off at the corner of 2nd Street, right next to the movie theater. The diner should be a short walk from here. The place feels like its stuck in the past, framed by a single mountainside that's swathed in mist. I check the time. Then I cross the street and find the glowing sign of Twede's Cafe. There's something familiar about this place. Maybe it's just the vibe that all diners share.

Ben should already be waiting inside. It's a shorter trip for him, especially since he drove here. I pause at the entrance and take a breath to calm my nerves. Then I grab the door handle. For some reason, it's locked. I try it again, but it doesn't open. This must not be the right entrance. I walk around the building, but there doesn't seem to be another way to get inside.

I glance through the window. The sunlight reflecting off the glass makes it hard to see. It doesn't look like anyone's in there. There's a paint bucket on the floor by the cash register. Are they closed for renovation or something? Maybe I went to the wrong location. I check the address again. Then I send Ben a message.

> Just got off the bus

> Not sure if I'm at the right place

Where'd you go?

> Twede's cafe. But I think it's closed

That's the right place. I'm sitting at table inside

I check the door *again*. Still locked.

> This is embarrassing

> But I can't get inside

What do you mean?

> I think the door is broken

Oh

Let me come get you

A few minutes go by. Nobody opens the door. I send Ben another text.

> wya?

Outside

Where did you go?

I'm right in front of the door

> I don't see you

That's weird

Are you sure you're at the right place?

There must be another entrance somewhere. I walk to the other side of the diner, but I still don't see him anywhere. This has to be the wrong location.

> Can you send the address again?

> Maybe I put it in wrong

Ben sends it, but it's the same one. There must be some mistake.

> I'm so confused right now

> What cross street are you at?

> North Bend Way and Bendigo

I look out at the street signs. NORTH BEND WAY and BENDIGO. This is the right place. So why can't we find each other?

> That's where I am too

> But I still don't see you anywhere

Should I try the door one more time? I take another glance around me. There's not a single car in the parking lot. And I haven't seen anyone walk in or out yet. As I'm standing there, waiting for him to respond, a thought occurs to me . . .

Maybe Ben isn't here at all. Is that why I can't seem to find him? This is all some practical joke that's being played on me. My heart sinks as I think back to these past few weeks. Does that mean everything he said is a lie?

I can't believe I came all the way here. Just to walk in circles, searching for someone who's never coming. Now I have to wait for the next bus home. I send him one last message.

> Very funny joke

> I'm leaving now

> Hope you had a nice laugh

Should have known better than to get my hopes up. As I'm walking off, he messages me back.

> Wait what do you mean?

> I'm trying to find you

I don't respond. He texts me again.

> Please don't leave yet

> I really want to see you

> Not sure why I can't see you

I stare at his message. I really want this to be true. I mean, I've been looking forward to seeing him, too. My fingers hover over the screen, thinking about what to text back. Then I decide to call him instead.

As the phone starts ringing, the sound of static breaks through, followed by a strange shift in the air. At first, I think the call was lost.

Then I hear a voice behind me.

"Oliver?"

I turn around slowly.

Someone is standing a few feet away, wearing a dark brown jacket and jeans. His black hair is bathed in golden light. I've only seen him in a few photos online. But I know it's Ben, staring right back at me.

CHAPTER SIX

A breeze blows in from behind him, ruffling the waves in his hair. There's a silence as we take each other in for the first time. Finally, I remember to say something.

"Ben?"

"*Hey*," he breathes, almost with relief.

I can't believe it's actually him. Standing in front of me.

"I'm sorry about the text, I thought—" I start.

"It's alright," he says. "Not sure how we missed each other."

"Yeah, me neither."

Ben smiles. "Glad I finally found you."

The neon sign blinks above our heads. He's a little taller than I expected, more handsome than his photo. He nods toward the diner and says, "Are you ready to head inside?"

"Uh, yeah."

I follow him to the door I tried earlier. I'm expecting it

to be locked. But for some reason, it opens easily for him. Maybe I was pushing it the wrong way? Ben holds the door, letting me go in first. Red barstools line a countertop that runs down the center of the room. There are a few people sitting inside, too.

Ben leads me to an empty booth near the back. As we take a seat, a woman comes to hand us our menus. I notice the silver ring on his index finger. We both are quiet for a moment, glancing down at our menus. Maybe he's a little nervous as well. Eventually, he asks, "Do you like coffee?"

"Not really, but my friend told me it's an acquired taste."

"This place might not change your mind."

"Well, not with that attitude," I say.

We both chuckle. I look back down at the menu. It's hard not to keep staring at him though. The person I've been texting all this time. Here we are, finally meeting in person. He must have noticed, because he leans back and says, "Do I look like what you expected?"

"Maybe a little taller. But I didn't have much to go off of."

"I probably should have sent a photo."

"I like the surprise."

Ben smiles. "I do, too."

The woman returns and sets down some waters. I glance around the diner, taking in the checkered floors, the dated wood paneling. "I swear, this place looks so familiar."

"Have you ever seen *Twin Peaks*?" Ben asks. "It was filmed here."

"You mean, this diner?"

"The whole town, actually."

I glance out the window as scenes from the show fill my mind. "Oh my god, it totally was. The mountain and everything."

"I was hoping you were a fan," he says, smiling across the table. "See that barstool over there? It's the same one Agent Cooper sat on."

"*Get out.*"

"I think the mugs are original, too."

"I'm taking one home."

We hold in our laughs as the woman returns to take our order. I follow Ben's lead and ask for a deluxe cheeseburger and a "damn fine" cup of coffee. Thankfully, she understands the reference. And likely tired of it, too.

Ben takes me in from across the table. Eventually, he says, "I'm really glad you showed up. I was worried you might cancel."

"Of course not."

"Hopefully the drive here wasn't bad."

"It was great. Had my driver take the scenic route." I take a sip of water. "You have a car, right?"

Ben nods. "It's my dad's, but yeah. I like long drives though. You get to zone out and listen to music. Played some Velvet Underground on the way here."

"You really are a fan."

"I mean, aren't you?"

"Yeah. I was just listening to them, too. On the bus, I mean." I leave out the fact that I only made it through two songs.

"What's your favorite album?"

Oh god. "Uh, the first one?"

Ben nods. "That is their most popular. Do you have a favorite song?"

What's with these questions about the band? I'm about to

make up a title, but maybe I should tell the truth. After all, I want him to know the real me, right? I release a breath and say, "I have to be honest with you. I don't really like them."

Ben tilts his head. "What do you mean?"

"I mean, I've *tried*. It's just not for me. At all."

There's a brief silence. Then he breathes a sigh of relief. "Honestly, thank god. Because they're not for me, either."

"I thought you were a fan."

"Not exactly."

"But you sent me all those videos."

"Because I thought you liked them," he explains.

"No! I only watched because I thought *you* liked them."

It takes a moment for this to sink in. Then we both crack a smile, realizing what we've done.

"Wait a second," Ben says, holding his hands up. "This doesn't make sense. What about that song you asked about?"

"It's the only one I know from them. Only because Sam used to play it," I explain. "I just couldn't remember the name."

"So *he* was the fan?"

I nod. "Yeah. He and I never had the same taste in music. But it reminds me of him. That's why I wanted to listen to it again."

"Sure you had other things in common," he says.

"Like you?"

Ben blinks at me. "What do you mean?"

"Your phone number. Remember?"

"*Right*. I almost forget about that."

"It's weird to think about, huh? The reason we're sitting here."

Ben nods. "It does make an interesting origin story."

"Definitely," I agree. "Never thought I'd meet someone through my dead friend's phone number."

"Do you still have it saved under his name?"

I hesitate. "Of course not."

Ben gives me a suspicious look. "Prove it."

"Alright, fine—"

I pull up our messages. Then I turn my phone around.

Sam (Also Ben)

He squints at the screen. "You know what? I'll take that."

I sigh. "I can change it . . ."

"It's alright," Ben says with a shrug. "You don't have to right now. I mean, it did belong to him first. And I know how much he meant to you."

It's really nice of him to say. Part of me wonders what Sam would think about all this. In a strange way, he brought us together. Just like he did with me and Julie. I fold my arms on the table and say, "You want to hear a story about him? There was this girl he was dating. I didn't really like her at first. For months, we'd be in the same room and barely say a word to each other. After Sam died, I didn't know who else to talk to. I figured she probably missed him, too. So I showed up at her house one night and threw rocks at her window. And we've been best friends ever since."

Ben smiles. "I'm glad there's a silver lining."

"Yeah. Sadly, she's studying abroad right now."

"Copenhagen, right?"

I blink at him. "Did I mention Julie already?"

Ben thinks about it. "It might have been from one of your messages when you were still texting Sam . . ."

I keep forgetting about those messages. I must have sent hundreds of them. Ben has read some of my deepest thoughts;

he knows things I've never told anyone else. But I'm only getting to know him now. I look at him and say the quiet part out loud. "I forgot how much you already know about me."

"I suppose that's true. Hopefully, that's not weird."

"I wouldn't say weird," I answer. "After all, I was the one messaging you. But it gives you an unfair advantage, if you know what I mean."

"You're right about that." He leans back, crossing his arms. "Why don't you ask me some questions, then. To even out the playing field. Anything you want to know."

"Anything?"

Ben nods. "It's only fair, right?"

"Okay, I like this idea." I rub my chin, thinking of some questions. "Let me start with an easy one. What's your favorite color?"

"Green."

"Like light green, or dark green, or—"

"More like the color of your eyes," he says, smirking.

I hold back a smile. "Do you have siblings?"

"It's just me. Though I always wanted a twin."

"Would you be the good twin or evil one?"

"Obviously the good one."

"Hmm. That's something an evil twin would say . . ."

The waitress arrives with our food. Ben takes a sip of coffee. Then he sets it down and says, "Next question. And feel free to get more personal."

"Alright. Where do you see yourself in ten years?"

"My parents want me to be a software engineer," he says, running a hand through his dark hair. "Which wouldn't be the end of the world. But my goal is to work for an observatory. Or even become a professor, if I don't get sick of school."

"Are you close with your parents?"

He nods. "I'd say so. Maybe more with my dad."

"Have you always lived in Bellevue?"

"I actually grew up in Sacramento. My family moved when I was fourteen."

"What's your deepest regret?"

His brows slightly raise. "That's quite the jump."

"Give me an honest answer, too. Not how you wish you got better grades or something like that."

"What if it's a little depressing?"

"*Ben.*" I give him a look. "I've been texting my dead best friend for a year. Doesn't get more depressing than that."

"Okay, you're right." Ben stares at the table, taking his time with this one. "Well, if you want an honest answer, I wasn't always an only child. I had an older brother. His name was Peter. He was a few years older than me. We weren't exactly the closest growing up. I didn't speak to him much after he left for college." He looks at me again. "That's probably my biggest regret. Not making an effort to talk to him. Send a text here and there. I wish I had picked up the phone and called him sometimes. I never thought there'd be a day I couldn't anymore."

"I'm sorry about that."

"It's alright," he says. "It's been a few years."

"Doesn't mean it hurts less."

"There are harder days for sure," he admits.

"I know the feeling."

He looks at me. "Can I ask you about Sam?"

"Sure."

"How long were you two friends?"

"Since seventh grade."

"That's a long time," he says.

"We were best friends. I'm sure you got that from my texts."

"I did."

Another question pops into my head. "How come you didn't just block me?"

"Why would I block you?"

"Because of all my text messages," I say. "It must have been annoying, right? You could have blocked me at any point. But you didn't."

"I might have considered it at first," he admits. "Then I realized why you were sending them. I figured you needed the space to talk to him again. I didn't want to take that away from you."

It definitely would have hurt if the messages couldn't go through. "I appreciate that," I say.

Ben smiles a little. "And if we're being honest, it was nice to hear from someone. Even though I didn't know who it was. Your messages came when I was feeling alone. I thought about texting you back a few times. Of course, I never did."

"You must have been surprised when I called."

"You could say that . . ."

"What was going through your mind, when you saw the number?"

"I figured it was an accident," he says, shrugging. "But a small part of me thought you might have needed someone to talk to."

"So you picked up."

"Yeah. I did."

We smile at each other. A few weeks ago, I didn't know someone was on the other end. Now here we are, sitting at the same table. The truth is, I did need someone to talk to. I just never expected it to be him. It sounds like he might have needed someone, too. Ben takes the first bite of his burger. We share some fries and order milkshakes for dessert. Hopefully, we'll get to come here again one day.

It's dark when we leave the diner. Streetlamps illuminate the sidewalk as Ben walks me to the bus stop. I wish we could hang out a little longer, but the last bus leaves at nine fifteen. I told Ben he doesn't have to wait with me, but he does anyway.

"Thanks again for the invite," I say.

Ben smiles at me. "I'm glad you came. I had a really good time. Hope the place lived up to your expectations."

"Yeah, it felt like being on the show. I wish I had taken something as a souvenir."

"*Actually* . . ." Ben pulls out a pen from his pocket. "I accidently grabbed it after we signed the check. But I'm sure they won't miss it. Here, something to remember the night."

I turn the pen in my hand. The letters "RR" are written on the side of it, which is the name of the diner from the show. "Thank you. I'll remember to steal something for you next time."

"Hopefully, that's your way of saying you want to see me again."

I smile. "Of course it is."

I think about asking him what his plans are next weekend, but headlights appear down the road. The bus has arrived a few minutes early. The doors open, but I don't want to go yet.

"Thanks for waiting with me," I say.

"Don't mention it. Let me know when you make it back, okay?"

We hug each other goodbye. Then I climb inside the bus. Ben doesn't head back to his car right away. He stands at the corner, hands in his pockets, watching the bus drive off.

The moment he disappears from view, I rest my head against the glass. I know this is the first time we've met in person, but I'm starting to miss him already. I close my eyes and replay the night in my head.

CHAPTER SEVEN

Julie calls me first thing in the morning. We've been trying to schedule it all week. The time difference has been a challenge. My days start when hers are just ending. It's almost like time traveling, if you think about it. It's been a few days since I met Ben in person, and I've been waiting to tell Julie over the phone.

"Surprised you answered the phone this early," she says.

"It's only ten thirty."

"Don't you usually sleep until noon?"

"Did you call to lecture me?"

"One second—" There's a brief silence, followed by some background noise. "Sorry, had to put in my earbuds. Can you hear me?"

"Yeah, where are you?"

"Walking back to my place," Julie says. "Just left wine night with some friends from the program. I didn't drink anything though."

"How are the people there?"

"Everyone's been nice," she says. "At least to my face anyway. You know how they feel about Americans. Someone even asked me if I owned a gun."

"Well, *do you?*"

"You're hilarious. Actually, that reminds me. There's this guy in my program from Boston who reminds me of you. He has the exact same sense of humor—and he shows up late to everything. We've been hanging out almost every day. I was actually just with him."

"So you've replaced me already . . ."

"Don't be ridiculous. You would honestly love him. He's so much fun."

I lie back on the bed and groan. "That's not what you're supposed to tell me. You're supposed to say you're having a miserable time and you're booking the next flight home."

"We're supposed be manifesting *nice* things, Oliver."

"It would be *nice* if you came home."

Julie sighs. "I'm hanging up."

"*Alright, alright.* I'm glad you're making new friends, okay?"

"Was that so hard? Now tell me about you. How's my mom's class?"

I think about this. "It's been . . . *interesting.*"

"Doesn't sound like a glowing review."

"No, she's great," I assure her. "It's honestly better than my other classes. But it can get a little confusing. She always answers our questions with another question."

"Sounds like my childhood."

"I wish I had that growing up." I switch the phone to my

other ear. "Did you know there are no due dates in her class? You can turn in assignments whenever you want."

"Mom doesn't believe in deadlines," Julie explains. "But I wouldn't take advantage of it. I think a lot of her past students have."

"Who said I was taking advantage of it?"

"Have you started the first assignment?"

I hesitate. "No . . ."

"*Oliver.*"

"I'm going to, okay? Give me a break. I had a busy weekend."

"What were you up to?"

I was waiting for us to get to this. Julie usually knows everything that's going on in my life, so I can't keep this secret for long.

"That's actually what I wanted to tell you. I sort of met someone."

"As in, a boy?"

"Maybe."

"What's his name?"

"It's Ben."

"*Ben,*" she repeats. "Does he go to our school or . . ."

"No. Thank god."

"How did you two meet?"

I obviously can't tell the truth. "We met on an app."

"Oh . . ."

"*Not that one!*"

"I wouldn't judge you if it was."

"Well it wasn't, okay?"

Julie chuckles. "Well, tell me about him. Is he cute?"

"Of course he is."

"How long have you guys been talking?"

"A couple of weeks."

"And you didn't tell me?"

"I wasn't sure what the vibe was," I say, sitting up again. "And we've only met up once. Just a couple days ago."

"How was it?"

I tell her about our dinner, the conversation we had, the questions I asked him. How he waited at the bus stop with me afterwards. "And we text each other every day, which is a good sign."

"Does that mean you like him?"

"Maybe. But I don't want to jinx it."

There's a pause before Julie says, "I think that's a good approach. Especially after what happened with you-know-who. But don't let that hold you back from opening up more. When are you going to see him again?"

I sigh. "One thing I haven't mentioned yet—he lives in Seattle."

"Oh . . . that's not ideal."

"I know . . ."

"I'm sure you could make it work," she says.

Navigating a long-distance relationship is something I've been thinking about. But I shouldn't be getting ahead of myself. After all, we've only met up once. "Maybe it wasn't even a real date. For all I know, he just wants to be friends."

"Would you be okay with that?"

I think about it. "I guess so."

"Good. Because I don't want you to get hurt again."

"I'll be fine."

After all, we're still getting to know each other. How could I possibly get hurt if nothing's happened? And it's not like he lives in *Copenhagen* or something. We can always continue meeting in the middle. I appreciate Julie's concern, though.

We stay on the phone for another hour or so. I could honestly talk with her for hours, asking questions about her daily life, the restaurants she's been to. But eventually I have to let her go.

"I have to hop in the shower and get ready for bed," she says.

"Alrighty. Have a good night."

"I'll text you in the morning."

I hang up and stretch my arms. I don't have to be in class for a few hours. But maybe I should learn to start my day sooner. Ben is probably in the lab right now. He texted me a couple hours ago.

> Morning.

> Hope you have a good start to your day

It's nice having something to wake up to. It's nice having *someone* to wake up to.

I'm still thinking about the question Julie asked me. *Of course* I would stay friends with him. Why would I want to lose someone like Ben?

* * *

The school week goes by slowly, but working the circulation desk is a nice break from my classes. Rami is really growing on me. We'll often have lunch together now. He showed me the secret staff lounge with an espresso machine.

"Why didn't you bring me here sooner?" I ask.

"I didn't know if I could trust you yet."

Even better, he's also a musical theater person. We listen to the *Wicked* soundtrack while we're working the desk together. Usually, I stay in the library for a few hours after my shifts. But I can't find an open table this afternoon. Maybe I'll head to the dining hall or something. I could use a snack anyway.

As I'm cutting through the quad, I spot him immediately.

Nolan is sitting in the grass with some friends. Those bleach blond waves always stick out in a crowd. It's been a few weeks since he showed up at my dorm. Thankfully, he hasn't made a second visit. Then, I notice someone else. Connor is sitting right beside him. The same Connor that Nolan cheated on me with. What are they even doing together? Nolan told me he was never going to speak to him again. *That liar.* I should walk over there and confront him about it. But Nolan and I aren't together anymore. So this shouldn't bother me. I turn around before either of them sees me standing here.

I wish I could teleport to Copenhagen. Julie would be able to talk me through this. Who cares if they're sitting together? Maybe they deserve each other anyway. I push them out of my mind as I head toward the student center. The second floor is usually less crowded. I find an empty table by the window.

I take a deep breath in and try to focus on something else. Maybe I'll start on the assignment from Professor Clarke. It doesn't sound too hard. All we have to do is open *The Poetics of Space* to a random page and start writing about it. I pull out my copy and read until I find a passage that grabs my attention.

I can recover my calm by living the metaphors of the ocean.

I say it out loud a few times. Is this book telling me to jump into the ocean? I continue reading, trying to figure out what it means. But it doesn't really make sense to me.

So I turn to another page and find a different passage. Somehow, this one is even *more* confusing. The author is going on about dreams and furnishing a house or something. It feels like I'm missing a lot of context. I wish I could just start from the beginning. How am I supposed to understand anything when I don't know what happened before?

I'm skimming other passages when I get a message from Ben.

> Amélie was amazing

> You have to see it

He's been telling me about this French course he's taking. Apparently, they get to watch a different French film every week and then analyze it together. Sounds a lot more fun than most of the classes I'm taking. If he didn't live so far away, maybe we could watch them together.

> Isn't it in French?

> That's what subtitles are for

> How's that book you're reading btw

I told him about the assignment earlier. He's been very curious about it.

> Honestly nothing is making sense so far

> Give me an example

I open the book to another page and pick a random line.

> "Inhabited space transcends geometrical space"

Wow

That hurt my brain a little

          Now you know how I feel

What's this book called again?

          The Poetics of Space

Sounds like an astronomy textbook

          For all I know, it could be

Maybe it's talking about black holes

          What makes you think that?

They're geometrical and transcend time and space

Just throwing it out there

          That kinda makes sense. Apparently there are no wrong answers. But I'm not an astronomy major so I don't know much about space

> I could send you some articles

That'd be great

Something with pictures would be lovely

> If you want pictures, I can show you in person

> With a telescope

Really?

> We have an observatory on campus

> I have a key so we could go anytime

I've been waiting for the chance to see him again.

I would love that

We share our schedules over the next few days. Thankfully, the weekend forecast is showing clear skies. So we decide to meet each other on Saturday. He's watching another French film for his class that evening and asks if I want to join. The showing is at six o'clock at his local theater.

> Can't wait to hang out again

Me too

I can't stop smiling at his message. A movie showing,

followed by stargazing. Is this considered a date? How am I supposed to focus on anything else until then? I can't wait get Julie's thoughts about this.

Mom has been working a lot this week, so we decide to do takeout for dinner. I pick up some Chinese food on the way home. There's this hole-in-the-wall place called King's Dragon that we always order from. We haven't had it in ages. Mom loves their lo mein and sesame chicken.

"Knock, knock," I say, entering the apartment. It's dark in the living room. I'm about to turn on the light when I spot her sleeping on the sofa with the television on. I would wake her up for dinner, but I know how tired she must be. She worked a double shift the night before. So I put a blanket over her and set the food on the kitchen table.

There are some dishes in the sink. I wash them quietly and put them on the rack to dry. Then I take out the trash, along with the recycling. Mom is still asleep when I come back inside. I wish she didn't have to work so much.

I glance around our small apartment. I'm not exactly the son you can brag about. Yet the walls are decorated with my graduation cap, drawings from kindergarten, photos of me growing with every grade. It makes me want to do better in school. Maybe I can buy us a real house one day.

"*No matter what, we have each other*," she always says.

I put the Chinese food in the fridge and turn off the television. Then I give her a kiss on the forehead and make my way out.

CHAPTER EIGHT

Someone pulls the fire alarm in the library again. It's the second time that's happened since I started working there. Rami and I have to wait outside until the fire department arrives. Why couldn't they have the decency to do this during the school week, instead of on a Saturday afternoon when I'm supposed to meet Ben in an hour. I send him a message, letting him know I'm running late.

No rush. I'll see you soon

Save me some popcorn

Extra butter

Something to drink?

> Diet soda please. And nachos if they have it

> I'll sneak it in if they don't

We were supposed to grab some food before the movie, but I'm going to have to meet him at the theater. I run home to change into the outfit I picked out last night. Then I race to the bus station. It's a smooth ride until we hit some traffic on the 405. Thankfully, we're only twenty minutes behind schedule. I run all the way to the theater.

The trailers have already started when I finally arrive. Ben texted me a moment ago, letting me know he's sitting inside. I buy a ticket and find the auditorium. I head through the door and glance up at the seats. Surprisingly, the place is almost full. I can't seem to spot Ben, so I send him another text.

> Where are you sitting again?

> Middle section on the right

I take another look around. But I still can't find him.

> I don't see you

> I'll wave at you

I scan the theater again. No waving hands. Did I walk into the wrong auditorium? I head out and try the next one. But it's not the right movie.

I get another text from Ben.

> It's auditorium 3

Wasn't that the first one I tried? I probably just didn't see him through the dark. I return to where I started, but something is different this time. There are only about ten people in here. I could have sworn the room was almost full a minute ago. But I don't think about it for long, because I spot Ben right away this time. He's sitting in the middle, waving at me. How did I miss him before? I take the seat next to him.

"*You made it,*" he whispers.

"Got confused for a second."

Ben smiles. "Don't worry. You didn't miss much."

Up on the screen, a woman is waiting outside a restaurant in Paris. She's putting on lipstick when a man in a suit approaches her, carrying flowers. "*Est-ce qu'elles sont pour moi?*"

Ben hands me the popcorn and whispers, "*That's her fiancé, by the way, but I think he's about to break up with her.*"

"At least he brought her flowers."

"Carnations though?"

"You're right. She should be breaking up with *him*."

We must be talking too loudly, because someone shushes us from behind. Ben and I lean back and try not to laugh. At least the movie has subtitles, but I don't need a translation to know this is not something I would ever watch on my own. Ben keeps looking over to check if I'm enjoying it. I smile to let him know I'm not bored. It doesn't really matter what I'm watching with him. Because I'm with *him*.

At one point in the film, my hand accidently touches his. Neither of us pulls away. For a second, I think about lacing my fingers through his. Maybe that's too much too soon. But then he leans his shoulder against mine. I can't tell if he's doing this intentionally. Regardless, I don't move away. We sit this way—hands touching, shoulders pressed together, my heart pounding—for the rest of the movie.

There's too much light out to look at the stars right now, so Ben takes me to his favorite pizza place. It's only a few blocks away and he gives me a tour of the neighborhood on the walk over. The streets are crowded with college students drinking outside of dive bars. Ben grabs us two slices of cheese pizza and a side of ranch, which I consider a green flag. Now that we're outside, I can get a better look at him. His hair looks freshly cut and his cheeks are slightly rosy from the cold air. He looks at me and says, "Sorry about the movie."

"What do you mean? I *loved* it."

He raises a brow. "You fell asleep at the end."

"Me, *asleep*?" I scoff. "No, no. I closed my eyes to better hear the dialogue."

"I didn't realize you were fluent in French."

"Oui," I say, and then I take a bite of pizza. "There's a lot you don't know about me. But I get to pick the next movie."

Ben smirks. "That's only fair."

"Why are you taking this class again? Thought you were an astronomy major."

"I thought it would fun," he says. "You only get so many electives. Don't want to spend every second of my life in a lab, you know? My brain would probably explode. Besides, I'm on track to graduate a year early anyway."

"And here I am, wondering if I'm even *going* to graduate."

Ben laughs. "You just haven't figured out what you like yet. Who knows, maybe tonight will give you some inspiration."

"As in, be an astronomy major?"

"It's a possibility," he says, winking at me. "I'll do my best to convince you."

"You did convince me to sit through a two-hour French movie."

"I thought you said you liked it."

"Not liked," I correct him. "*Loved.*"

We laugh and finish the rest of our pizza. Then Ben takes me to a famous bakery in town. The place is extra crowded tonight, but the pastry selection makes everything worth it. I can't decide what to get.

"Best cannoli in the world," Ben says.

"I would normally argue with that, but my favorite bakery in Ellensburg just closed down. I'm still grieving, actually."

Ben places his hand on my shoulder. "We'll order some in its memory. And a cinnamon roll while we're here."

We pay at the register and head outside again. The temperature has suddenly dropped, making me shiver a little. That's when I realize I forgot something. "*Wait. My jacket.*"

"Did you lose it?"

"Yeah!" I think back to the places we've been. I don't remember bringing it to the movie. "I must have left it on the bus." I let out a long breath. Now I'll have to call lost and found in the morning.

"Here, you can wear mine." He removes his jacket for me.

"Then you'll be cold."

"I'll be fine, I'm wearing a thick sweater."

He places his jacket around my shoulders. It carries the warmth of him, feeling like an embrace. I take in the scent of his cologne. Hopefully, I'm not blushing too hard when I say, "That's really nice of you."

Ben just smiles at me. He leads us toward the center of campus, and the university clock tower rises into view. The quad is more than twice the size of CWU. I would probably get lost in the maze of trees if I walked through here alone. Thankfully, I have Ben to show me around.

Apparently, he doesn't have access to the observatory this weekend. "Don't worry, I have a plan B," he says. To be honest, it doesn't really matter where we're heading. We could sit on the sidewalk and I would enjoy it all the same.

Eventually, we reach the entrance of an old brick building as he takes out his key card. "This is the astronomy department," he says, unlocking the door. "We're not really supposed to be here this late, but my TA let me borrow his key."

"So we're sneaking in?"

"Let's not use that word," he whispers.

Since it's a Saturday night, the place is vacant of students. At first, I think he's going to show me something in his lab. But we take the elevator to the top floor. There's a stairwell at the end of the hallway. We climb to the top and Ben pushes open a metal door. A breeze rolls through as he leads me onto the rooftop. I glance over the ledge, taking in the view of the city.

There's a blanket laid out in the middle of the roof. Next to it is a telescope that's angled toward the night sky. Ben walks over to it and says, "I set this up earlier for us. Just have to adjust a few things."

"Did you borrow it from the department?"

"It's actually mine," he says, running a proud hand over it. "It was my graduation present. My parents said it was this or a trip to Greece."

"You turned down a trip to Greece?"

"I like to use the word *postponed*. It's all about how you frame things, you know?"

I nod thoughtfully. "Well, in that sense, I've also *postponed* a trip to Greece."

"Maybe we'll end up going together." He smiles at me again. Then he bends down, twisting a metal knob beneath the lens. A moment later, he lifts back up and says, "Alright, it's ready for you."

Ben explains the right technique. Apparently, you have to keep both eyes open when you're looking. And you can't stand too close or you won't see things clearly.

It takes a second for the image to focus. Small pinpricks of light shine through a dark sky. "So what am I looking at?"

"See the white speck in the center? That's the Orion Nebula."

"That small smudge of light?"

"Exactly. It's one of the closest star-forming regions to Earth," he explains. "You can see it with the naked eye in the wintertime, but it's not as clear without a telescope. And see the three bright stars on the right? That's Orion's Belt."

It looks like a string of pearls in a dark sky. "How far away is it?"

"About fifteen hundred light-years."

"Oh, wow."

"Let me show you something else—"

I step back and Ben adjusts the telescope again. He seems more excited for me to see this one. As I lean forward to look, he places a hand on my back, which makes me go still. For a second, I forget what I'm supposed to be doing.

"That's Coma Berenices constellation," he says. "It probably looks like a bunch of stars at first. But each one is an actually an entire galaxy."

"Those are *galaxies*?"

"Thousands of them, actually."

"But they're so small . . ."

"They're millions of light-years from here. The interesting thing is we're actually seeing them from the future," he says.

"What do you mean?"

"It takes time for light to travel to us. So what we're seeing now is light being emitted from millions of light-years away," he explains. "Which means we're looking at these objects as they were millions of years ago. There's a chance they might not even exist anymore. Or other galaxies could have been born. A telescope is sort of like a time machine that way. You don't really see things as they are now."

I take this in for a second. "So what you're saying is, I'm actually looking into the past?"

"Exactly."

I take another look through the telescope. "What's this one called again?"

"The Coma Berenices. Or more affectionately, Berenice's Hair."

"How did they come up with that?"

"It's named after Queen Berenice II of Egypt," he says. "After her husband went off to fight in the war, she sacrificed her hair to Aphrodite for his safe return."

"Her hair must have been beautiful."

"They did name a constellation after it."

Our faces are close to each other. His skin is soft in the pale light. Somehow, I find the confidence to brush his hair to the side and say, "You know, I'd name one after you, too."

Ben's lips curve into a smile. "Is that so?"

"And what about me?"

He takes me in. "I'd name one after your eyes."

I look at him, then at his lips again. For a second, I think about kissing him. I wonder if he's thinking the same thing. Maybe I let too much time pass, because Ben turns back to adjust the telescope. I love seeing how passionate he is about all this. It reminds me of Julie and her writing.

"How often do you come up here?"

"Not as much as I'd like," he says.

"What's your favorite part about it?"

"My favorite part?" Ben thinks about it for a moment. "Probably the slim chance that I could discover something new. It's why I started taking astronomy classes. There's so much of the universe we haven't explored yet, you know? And the more we find out, the more we realize how little we actually know about it. We're always open to being proven wrong. Think about a cup of water compared to the ocean. That's as much of the universe as we've actually explored. Which is really nothing at all." He looks up at the sky and adds, "Maybe I'll never discover anything. But I enjoy the possibility that I might."

I follow his gaze, trying to see what he's looking at. It makes me want to find something I'm this passionate about, too. "If we know nothing about the universe, then the chance of you discovering something isn't really slim at all," I figure. "If anything, it means it's even *more* likely."

Ben tilts his head a little. "That's a nice way of looking at it."

"It's all about how we frame things, right?"

"Exactly."

We both smile at this. Then Ben shows me more planets

and his favorite constellations. He shows me the moons of Saturn, which I never realized were made of ice. He also shows me Jupiter and the Great Red Spot that's shrinking.

Afterward, we sit on the blanket he set up earlier. Ben puts on some music from his phone, and we try the pastries. The cannoli are *almost* as good as the ones back home. I wish we could stay here and watch the sun come up together. But I have to make it on the last bus home. Eventually, we have to call it a night.

I help Ben pack his telescope and carry it outside. I offer to help him bring it back, even though his apartment is in the other direction. "It's alright," he assures me. "I don't want you missing the bus."

"Your jacket—" I'm about to take it off, but he holds up a hand.

"You can give it back later," he says.

"Are you sure?"

"Yeah." Ben nods. "It gives us an excuse to hang out again."

"You know we don't need an excuse for that." I offer another smile. Then I look at the time and say, "I should probably get going."

"Text me when you get back, alright?"

"For sure."

As we're hugging each other goodbye, I keep my arms around him longer this time. It's nice to feel him so close to me, his cheek warm against mine. But eventually we have to pull apart. Ben promises to make the trip to me next time. It would be nice to show him around Ellensburg. I spend the whole ride home thinking about all the places I'll take him.

CHAPTER NINE

"For our house is our corner of the world. As has often been said, it is our first universe." —Gaston Bachelard

Those words are written on the board when I come into class. It's Friday afternoon, which means there's only a few hours before the weekend starts. Professor Clarke is standing at the front, drinking from a Christmas mug. She waits for all of us be seated before she says, "Good afternoon, everyone. This week has truly flown by, hasn't it? I'm sure many of you have exciting plans for the weekend, but hopefully you haven't checked out just yet. Please ignore the mug I'm drinking from today. Everything else is in the dishwasher." She takes a sip from it and sets it down on the table. "I promise there's no deeper meaning behind it, in case you were wondering.

"Now on to today's class," she continues. "I've had the

chance to read the assignments you turned in this week. From what I can tell, most of you are enjoying the text we've been reading together. While each of you started somewhere different, it seems we have begun to encounter this image of a house, which Bachelard describes as *our first universe*." She pauses to let the words sink in. "What do you suppose he means by this?"

A girl in the front eventually raises her hand. "I think he's talking about how the home shapes our worldview," she says.

Professor Clarke nods. "Why, yes. It is the home that contains all of our first experiences—from our first steps to the first words we hear and speak—and those things do construct our very understanding of everything else. *But*, I think there's more he wants to say. He speaks of corners to hide in, drawers containing secrets, things lost within the attic." She looks around. "Anyone else?"

The guy next to me raises a hand. "I think the rooms are supposed to represent our imagination, right?"

"*Yes*. The imagination." She nods thoughtfully. "If you think about it, the house is what taught us to daydream. It is from the smallest spaces that our minds construct entire *worlds*. It's where we learn to imagine in the corner, alone. Especially as children, isn't that right? We might look at an empty room and see nothing, while a younger version of ourselves may see the possibility of everything. Now, Bachelard thinks this way of imagining has been forgotten. A sense of poetry that is lost once we leave the home." She pauses for emphasis. "Is this poetry something we can rediscover? That is, the ability for us to imagine without limits. I'd like us to think about this as we move on to today's activity . . ."

Professor Clarke has us free write for the first twenty

minutes. Then she breaks us into small groups to share our writing. I must have missed the memo, because everyone wrote about memories from their childhood, the homes they grew up in. Meanwhile, I wrote about the constellations I saw with Ben. I don't want to steer the conversation the wrong way. So I just stay quiet and listen to everyone else share their stories.

The class goes by slower than usual. But I hang around afterward to speak with Professor Clarke. I'm not sure if she noticed my lack of participation today, but I feel the need to explain myself anyway. She's wiping the board when I come up and say, "Sorry about my last assignment. I clearly misunderstood the word *space*."

"I don't know what you're apologizing for, Oliver. You know there are no wrong answers in this class."

"But everyone wrote about their home. And I chose to write about outer space."

Professor Clarke sets the eraser down. "The home is the mere embodiment of the imagination. So who's to stop you from writing about space itself?"

"I think I just made it more complicated for myself."

"And what makes that space more complicated?"

"Well, one is much *bigger* than the other," I say.

"I worry you may have missed the point." Professor Clarke looks at me. "Aren't the possibilities of a home, or what's inside of a single drawer, just as endless?"

I sigh. "No, I get that. The whole imagining part. But . . ."

"But what?"

I stare at the floor, unsure how to say this. "I was thinking about what you asked earlier. Why we lose that sense of ourselves when we leave the home. I feel like the answer's kind of obvious, right? You don't know what the world's really like when you're a kid. But then you grow up and realize it's nothing like you imagined. That not everything is possible, you know? And sometimes, you have to open the box and realize nothing's inside."

Professor Clarke grabs her bag from her desk and says, "I'm not going to disagree, as it's not my place to tell my students what to believe. Maybe a sense of wonder has no place in the world today." She looks at me again. "But let me say one thing about the limits we place on ourselves and our ideas of everything else: The key to imagining is to imagine otherwise."

I grab an iced coffee with extra sugar on my way to the library. I'm not scheduled to work today, but Rami should be in. Maybe I can hang with him for a couple hours. I settle in at the back room and take out *The Poetics of Space*. I don't usually start assignments on Friday afternoon, but Professor Clarke made me think about my current mindset. Maybe I should approach things differently. Everyone else seemed to enjoy recalling memories of their home. But what if you don't like the home you grew up in? I've blocked out the years we lived with my stepdad. The time before that wasn't exactly better. Mom and I moved around a lot growing up. The closest thing to a home is our current apartment that's too small for the both of us.

I stare at the blank screen for a while. Professor Clarke is right about my lack of imagination. Maybe I've always been this way. It's not like I had any big dreams growing up. I'm not a writer like Julie who always wanted to be a published author. Or a musician like Sam who dreamed of touring the world. Frankly, I never imagined anything beyond where I am right now. Getting through college so I can find a decent job. It's hard to imagine what's possible when you don't have much to start with.

The only interesting thing in my life is Ben. How we connected through Sam's old number. Maybe I should write about that instead. We're actually meeting later this afternoon. Ben is driving to Ellensburg this time. I've been looking forward to it all week.

Since Julie is in another time zone, I talk to him more than anyone else. Getting to know Ben feels so easy and natural. Even though we're always texting and keeping each other updated on our how our days are going, I'm constantly resisting the urge to send: *I miss you*. Hopefully, he misses me, too.

> Have you looked outside?

> There's a clear view of Orion's belt tonight

Was thinking about you too

Glad to see you interested in astronomy now

Eventually, Rami returns to the circulation desk. He was supposed to start his shift over an hour ago. I close my laptop and say, "And where exactly have you been?"

Rami sets down his sunglasses. "I was at Sweet Juice."

"You went to *lunch*?"

YOU'VE FOUND OLIVER

"Relax, it's Friday. People barely come to the library today. That's why I take this shift." He takes a seat in his usual chair, crossing one leg over the other. "What are you doing here anyway? I thought you were meeting that new boy."

"He's still on his way," I say.

"I'm so glad he's visiting you this time. It would have been a red flag if he made you take the bus to see him *again*."

"The bus isn't that bad."

"What kind of car does he drive?"

"Not sure."

"Hopefully something expensive. Like a Porsche."

I shrug. "You know I don't care about that."

Rami rolls his eyes. "Okay, Oliver Twist. As long as I'm invited to your wedding."

I lean back in my seat, sighing. "I still don't know if he likes me yet."

"Of course he likes you," Rami says. "He's not going to drive all the way from Seattle to be besties. He's probably wondering the same thing about you. You're not exactly the easiest person to read. Are you a water sign?"

I cross my arms. "I don't subscribe to astrology."

Rami looks at me. "That's something a Cancer would say."

My phone vibrates. There's a text message from Ben, saying he's here earlier than expected. I can't believe he's actually in Ellensburg right now.

Where should I park again?

Let me send you the location

> I'll meet you there now

I say goodbye to Rami and head out the door. It's another beautiful spring afternoon. Most of the cherry blossoms have fallen, covering the ground with petals. I have the whole day planned out for us. There's a river that runs the length of campus. You have to cross the bridge to get from the library to the south parking lot. Petals fall into the water as I'm walking over it. I text Ben, asking where he is.

> Near the language and literature building

I stop short. Because I was just coming from that direction. Maybe he crossed one of the other bridges? Then someone calls my name, making me turn around.

Ben is standing on the other side of the bridge, the side I came from, smiling at me. How did he get there so fast? I make my way over and embrace him with a hug. I feel his arms tighten around me. I wish I never had to pull away.

"You're almost an hour early," I say.

"Couldn't wait to see you again." He adjusts the bag over his shoulder. "It's also a curse of mine. I'm always early or the first to arrive."

"As long as you didn't run any red lights."

"Only a couple." He winks at me, obviously joking. Then he takes a look around and says, "You guys have a lot of bridges around here."

"I can give you the exclusive tour," I say. "But I was thinking we could grab coffee first. There's this place in town you'll like."

Ben smiles. "Can't wait to try it."

There's so many things I want to show him. Ellensburg might not be as big as Seattle, but there's still plenty to do around here. Sun and Moon is a short walk from campus. Thankfully, there's only a few people inside. We order our drinks and find a table in the back. Ben says the café reminds him of a coffee shop near his apartment. He glances at the hand-painted sign on the wall. "Sun and Moon," he says out loud. "Wonder how they came up with the name."

"Maybe the owner was an astronomy major," I say.

"Sounds like a better use of the degree." Ben takes a sip of his latte. "Have you ever thought about opening your own café?"

"I'm more of a donut shop guy."

Ben laughs. "That reminds me." He removes a small box from his bag and sets it on the table. I don't have to open it to know what's inside. "From the bakery we went to last weekend. I promised I'd bring you some more. You said your favorite place closed down, right? I couldn't show up without it."

"You remembered?" I take a look inside the box of pastries. There's even a chocolate croissant. "I actually have something for you, too. But I didn't bring it with me." I went back to the pottery place this week. I painted a cluster of stars on a tea plate. "I can grab it when we stop by my dorm."

"What is it?"

"You'll find out later. Just promise you won't hate it."

"I'm sure I'll love it."

We finish our drinks and make our way out. The temperature has cooled a little, but it's still a nice walk through downtown Ellensburg. Some of the shops have their doors open, displaying clothes on the sidewalk. We stop by my favorite record store and take a look around. Ben finds a *Born to Die* vinyl that's practically brand new. He thrifted a vintage record player a few months ago and is building a collection. I make a mental note of this for the future. Then we grab some ice cream across the street and continue our walk.

Ellensburg doesn't have much of an art scene, but there's a mural of a phoenix rising from the ashes outside of the Davidson Building. It symbolizes the rebuilding of the town after the Great Fire burned most of it down in 1889.

"How did the fire start?" Ben asks curiously.

"Phone charger. A real hazard back then."

Ben rolls his eyes and walks off. I love making him laugh. There are a few more shops we could check out, but I want to take him somewhere special. Especially after he took me stargazing on the rooftop. There's this endless golden field just outside of town. Julie took me there once before. I bet he's never seen the stars more clearly anywhere else. But there are more clouds today than I'd expected. So I'll save it for another time. Thankfully, I have another place in mind.

There's a dirt path at the end of the street, leading to the main hiking trail, but that's not where I'm taking us now. We go off the path, cutting through trees until it comes into view. Sunlight bounces off the mirror-like surface of the lake. It's been a long time since I've been back. Ben glances at the water and back at me. "I'm guessing this is your secret spot," he says.

"I'm trusting you'll keep it that way."

Sam and I used to spend the summers here, lounging on the grass. It doesn't take long for the memories to return. If I close my eyes for a second, I can hear his voice echoing through the air. Admittedly, it's a little strange to be here with

Ben instead, but I wanted to show him something different from the city views he's used to seeing. Ben stares at our reflection in the water. "Do you come here by yourself a lot?"

"It's actually been a while." I slide my hands into my pockets. "It's a lot nicer during the summer. I like to pretend it's my private lake in the Hamptons."

Ben smiles. "If only we could go for a swim."

I glance at the clouds above us. "I was hoping it would be warmer. Although I *have* jumped in when it was snowing."

"Oh, really?"

"It was an accident," I admit. "The lake froze over and I wanted to see if I could stand on it. Turns out I was . . . heavier than I thought."

"And how did you get out?"

"A friend was with me. I probably should have listened to him in the first place. He was pretty upset with me afterwards." I was sick in bed for a week, but I decide to leave that out.

"I'm guessing it was Sam."

"Yeah, it was. He was the one who showed me this place."

Ben nods and stares at the lake again. I stand beside him, taking in the world around us. I remember there being more flowers in the springtime. Maybe I'm misremembering things.

"My brother and I used to go hiking a lot," Ben says out of the blue. "Back when we lived in Sacramento. Sometimes, we went out way farther than we were supposed to. I remember finding a place that looked like this. I kinda forgot about that memory until now. Haven't thought about it in years."

"So you have your own secret lake?"

"Or maybe it's the same one," he says, looking at me.

"And we're just entering different portals to get there."

I think about it. "How would we test this theory?"

"I'll have to show you mine. So we can compare them."

"How scientific."

"It's been so long I hope I can find it again."

I smile at the thought of this. The two of us taking a trip together. I would honestly go anywhere with him. Maybe that's how you know you're falling for someone. When you don't care what the destination is.

We stare at each other for a long moment. His hair is almost glowing in the afternoon sunlight. I resist the urge to run my hand through it. I wish I had kissed him that night on the rooftop. Maybe this is my second chance to do it. I swallow my breath and lean forward—

But his phone goes off.

"Sorry, that's my alarm—" Ben turns it off.

"What's it for?"

"It's a reminder to look at my research fellowship application," he says. "But I'm practically done with it. It's with the European Space Agency. I'm hoping to work at this observatory in the Netherlands."

"That's sounds cool," I say.

"I didn't get it yet. But we'll see."

"I'm jealous you already know exactly what you want to do," I admit. "I can't even decide if I should sign up for a meal plan next quarter."

Ben slides his phone into his pocket. "I guess that's a nice way of looking at it. But there's always a trade-off, right?"

"What kind of trade-off?"

"For one, I didn't have any friends like Sam or Julie growing up," he says. "I spent most weekends alone studying in my room."

"Well, you're not alone anymore," I say. "Now you have me."

"I wish we didn't live far away."

"That hasn't stopped us so far, right?"

Ben smiles again. "No. It hasn't."

If we *were* going to kiss, the moment is gone. At least for right now. We still have the rest of the day together. I check the time on my phone. We should probably head back into town soon. I still need to give him a tour of campus. We hang around the lake for a moment longer. I hadn't really thought much about why I wanted to bring Ben *here*. But I think I just needed to see it again—and I didn't want to be alone. On our walk back, I turn to him and say, "I'm glad you came today. If I didn't mention that already."

"Wouldn't want to be anywhere else."

CHAPTER TEN

The drive-in restaurant is a staple in Ellensburg. It really adds to the small-town experience we have going on. Although most people just eat outside. Ben finds a table while I order for us—two cheeseburger combos with a basket of onion rings. I make him try the mystery milkshake flavor, which he thinks is piña colada. I don't tell him there's actually no mystery flavor—it's just vanilla. I still need to give him the gift I made. So we finish our food and head back to campus.

It's nice having someone to walk around with. In another world, we could spend every day together. I point out some more things along the way—the sculpture of the bull sitting on the bench; the street they close down for the farmer's market every Sunday; the sidewalk where Julie tripped and sprained her ankle last year. I even show him where my favorite bakery was before it closed down.

"Why are there people inside?" Ben asks.

"What people?"

At first, I think he's mistaken. Then I glance at the windows and notice the lights are on. Probably construction workers clearing things out. Then a young couple exits, carrying a familiar white box that's tied with a ribbon. That's when I catch the scent of something sweet. So we cross the street to check for ourselves.

The bell chimes as we enter the door. Some new bakery must have replaced it, because the place is up and running again. I take in the familiar wallpaper and the pastries that fill the display cases. They even have the same chocolate croissants. "I swear this place closed down a few months ago," I say.

"Maybe they were just remodeling," Ben guesses.

"But it looks exactly the same."

Same black-and-white checkered flooring. Same brick accent wall with the handwritten menu. A mother and daughter are picking out macarons at the counter. When they're finished paying, I approach the girl at the register. She smiles at me and says, "What can I get for you?"

"Hi, quick question. When did you guys reopen?"

"Reopen?"

"Yeah." I nod. "You were closed, right?"

"We close at seven," she says.

"No, I mean *closed down*."

"Closed down?"

"I saw the sign at the window," I tell her. "It said *thank you for thirty years of business*, or something like that. I thought that meant you were closed for good."

She looks confused. "Sorry, I just started here."

That's probably my cue to stop asking her questions. Maybe they're under new management or something.

Regardless, this is such great news. I have to text Julie about this. I would order something if Ben hadn't already brought pastries for us to share. So we make our way out again.

We cross the street and take the shortcut to campus. My dorm isn't the most impressive in the world. But at least we tend to keep the hallways clean. "My roommate is usually home around this time," I say. "You can just ignore him though."

"You two don't get along?"

"We're *cordial*," I explain. "But I wouldn't call him a friend. He won't let me light scented candles. *And* he plays loud country music. I still prefer him to my last one though."

"What happened to your last roommate?"

I sigh. "That's a story for later."

I stick my key into the doorknob. For some reason, it doesn't work. I wiggle it a few times, but it won't turn. So I knock on the door, hoping Ethan's inside. After a moment, a girl in a blue top opens it instead. She looks at me and says, "Can I help you?"

It seems Ethan has another "friend" visiting. He usually puts a rubber band on the doorknob. I wish he would tell me these things in advance. I take in a breath and say, "I just have to grab something."

"Grab what?" she asks.

"My stuff."

"What *stuff*?"

I'm not sure why I need to explain this to her. For some reason, she doesn't move out of the way for us. I'm suddenly annoyed by this exchange. But I don't want to be rude in front of Ben. So I try to move around her. "Excuse me."

"*What are you doing?*" She snaps.

"I need something from my room."

"This isn't your room."

"Yes, it is—"

"You can't just barge in—"

I'm not sure what Ethan told her. Maybe that he lives alone or something. "Fine. Just tell Ethan to grab my things for me."

"Who's Ethan?"

Ben looks at me. "Are you sure this is your room?"

"*Yes*. I live here."

"Is this some sort of prank?" the girl asks.

I don't have time for this right now. So I just force my way through, ignoring her loud protest. The second Ben comes inside, I push her out of the way and shut the door. "That was really annoying," I groan. "Sorry about that."

Then I glance around the room. It doesn't take me long to realize something's off. The flex wall that divides our beds is gone. And what happened to all of the furniture? There's an orange futon where the table should be. What's with these heart-shaped lights hanging along the ceiling? And who put the Harry Styles poster on the—

Then it finally hits me.

"Oh my god, this isn't my room," I gasp.

Ben's eyes widen. *"What?"*

There's a loud bang on the door. Followed by the girl shouting from the other side. "I'm calling campus police!"

"We should go—" I throw open the door again and pull Ben into the hallway. The girl continues shouting as we hurry out of the building. I'm so embarrassed, I take us all the way down the length of block until we're completely out of view. Thankfully, I don't think she followed us outside.

"So that was her room?" Ben asks.

"No, that should be my room! I mean, it's *supposed* to be."

"Are you sure it was the right building—"

"*Ben*. I've lived there for months. I was literally sleeping there this morning!"

I'm not sure how to make sense of this. All my things were missing. Did they move us out while I was gone? Maybe Ethan knows what's going on. I take out my phone to text him, but I can't find his number in my contacts.

Then I notice something else. There's something off about the trees. It takes me a second to realize . . . "What happened to the cherry blossoms?" I glance all around us. The ground was covered with petals this morning.

Ben blinks at me. "Why would there be cherry blossoms in the fall?"

"What do you mean *fall*? It's April."

"You think it's April?"

"What do *you* think it is?"

"November," he says.

"*November*? Ben, what are you talking about?"

He's obviously messing with me. Then I take another look at the trees. The leaves are curling at the edges as if they're about to fall. Everyone's walking around in boots and jackets. I turn abruptly and say, "I have to check something."

I make my way back to the quad. But there are no cherry blossoms here, either. As if someone swept them up with a magic wand. "Am I losing my mind? Where did all the petals go?"

Ben looks around. "Do you mean these trees?"

"*Yes*. You didn't see them earlier?"

"They don't bloom this time of year . . ."

"I know they peak in May. But there were still some this morning."

Ben raises his brow. "Wait, so you think we're in April?"

I'm not sure what calendar he's looking at. But this has to be a prank. I take out my phone to show him myself. Then I see the date on the screen. Something is definitely wrong here. "Why does it say *November*?"

I open up the calendar app. But it shows me the same thing. My heart pounds as I search through my phone. My photos and messages from the last few months are missing. The storage on my phone must not have updated. There has to be another way to check this. The bulletin board outside the student center. The date is always written above the list of activities. So I race over there immediately, pulling Ben along with me. When I see the Fall Festival flyers, my stomach drops. This has to be a dream or something. Those were taken down months ago.

My head is starting to spin. I nearly trip over as I turn around. Thankfully, Ben is there to catch my fall. "You look like you've seen a ghost," he says.

"Is it *really* November?"

"Why do you keep asking that?"

"Because it was April when I woke up."

Ben doesn't say anything. He just looks back at me with confusion. I take in the trees around us again. Is that why the cherry blossoms are gone? But I swear I saw some this morning. I'm trying my best not to lose it in front of Ben. I feel his hand on my shoulder as I clench my eyes shut, hoping everything goes back to normal. His voice is calming when he says, "Oliver . . . are you alright?"

"I think I'm going crazy."

"Maybe you should lie down."

My mind goes back to November. I was still living in my old dorm room. Is that why someone else is in my new one?

I don't understand how any of this is happening. If it's really six months ago, does that mean Julie is still here?

A thought occurs to me. I pull up her location on my phone. It's showing her on campus. What is she doing here?

CHAPTER ELEVEN

Julie is supposed to be thousands of miles away. So there's no way she should be here right now. I think about restarting my phone. I should just call her instead. The phone rings, but she doesn't answer me. I zoom in on her exact location. Apparently, she's right next to the library. I know this is likely some glitch. But I need to check it for myself.

I don't want to leave Ben here alone. So I grab his arm and say, *"Follow me—"*

Thankfully, the library isn't too far. It would be easier if she just answered the phone. Am I supposed to check every floor?

And then I see her, sitting at a table outside.

For a second, I think I'm imagining things. She's wearing her favorite bubblegum-pink cardigan. But she left for Copenhagen weeks ago. Does this mean it's really November again?

"*JULIE!*"

That came out much louder than I intended. Everyone around us turns to look at me. But I don't really care about that. I race toward her immediately.

"I thought she was studying abroad," Ben says.

"She's supposed to be!"

I don't even bother hiding my emotions. I throw my arms around her and shout, "Oh my god, it's really you!"

"Oliver, what's going on?" There's a flash of concern in her face.

"*I missed you.*"

"Missed me? I just saw you a few hours ago."

What does she mean? I haven't seen her in several weeks. But that doesn't matter right now, because I am just happy she's back. I squeeze her even tighter. That's when I notice the guy sitting next to her. He clears his throat.

Julie looks at him and says, "I'm sorry, Craig. This is my friend, Oliver." She turns to me. "Oliver, this is Craig."

I recognize him now. The tall guy from her creative writing class. They went on a few dates last quarter. We really must be back in the fall. Too bad Julie gets bored of him after their second date.

He gives me the bro nod. "Sup."

"Yeah, yeah." I don't have time for small talk. I turn back to Julie and say, "I really need to talk to you right now."

"About what?" She looks at Ben. "And who's this?"

"Oh. This is Ben."

Ben holds out his hand. "Nice to finally meet you. Oliver mentions you all the time."

"Oh?" She looks between us. "How do you two know each other again?"

I shake my head. "I'll tell you about him later, okay? I just need to talk to you right now."

"Is it important?"

"Yes."

"Are you sure it can't wait? I'm kind of busy right now." She gives me a look that says, *Can we do this another time?*

"But it's an emergency!"

"Is it a *real* emergency?"

As far as I'm concerned, it sure is. But I also don't want to ruin her date. I remember how much she was looking forward to this one. I guess I could just tell her in a few hours. Maybe that will give me time to figure this out. I let out a breath and say, "Okay, *fine*. Just call me after, okay?"

"Got it," she says.

I squeeze her shoulders. "Promise me."

"I will."

Ben smiles politely. "Lovely meeting again."

Julie looks at him. "Uh, you too."

"Let's go, Ben—"

We leave Julie alone with her date. She better call me as soon as it's over. Because I'm more confused than before. What on earth is going on here?

"They look like a nice couple," Ben says.

I sigh. "Don't get your hopes up. It's not going anywhere."

"How do you know that?"

"Because it already happened," I explain. "He's going to take her to a Mexican restaurant and ask to split the check."

Ben blinks at me. "What do you mean it already happened?"

Has he not been paying attention?

I place my hands on his shoulders and speak slowly. "Ben.

Where have you been these last few minutes? I told you. It's not supposed to be November right now. Please tell me you understand what I'm saying."

"I sort of do . . ." He goes quiet, maybe processing it. "Is that why Julie is still here?"

"Yes! Her program doesn't start until spring." My head pounds from trying to make sense of this. If we're back in the fall, that means I'm still living at my old place. "That's probably why my key didn't work earlier. I hadn't moved into the new dorm yet."

"So we really did break in . . ."

"I should check my old room."

We make our way back through campus. I'm surprised Ben is still tagging along with me. He must think I've gone crazy by now. As we're passing the student center, someone suddenly appears at my side. Then a hand moves around my waist, pulling me in for a kiss. Familiar lips feel warm against mine. It only takes a second to realize it's—

"*Nolan?*"

"Hey," he whispers.

"What do you think you're *doing*?"

"Did I scare you?" He smirks at me. "Though you were heading to Moore."

He tries to kiss me again, but I dodge it this time. "*Ew, stop that!*"

"Don't be so shy." He laughs.

I'm about to smack him for that—but I remember something. We're back in November. That means he and I haven't broken up yet.

Nolan checks his watch. "I'm actually on my way to the gym. But I'll see you tonight. Text me, okay?" He kisses me on the cheek before walking off.

I stand there for a second, completely mortified. I'm afraid to turn around and see Ben's reaction. There's a look of shock on his face. All I can think to say is "I'm sorry you saw that. . . ."

"Was that your . . ."

"Ex-boyfriend, yeah. I guess we haven't broken up, if it's November? That's probably why he thought it was okay to kiss me." It almost sounds worse when said out loud. I should have pushed him away sooner. But it's too late for that now. At least Ben doesn't seem too angry about it right now.

Eventually, we get to my old dorm building. It's across the street from the baseball field. My room is on the second floor.

"Do you have your old key?" Ben asks.

"We always left it unlocked."

We head upstairs and open the door. I see my plaid sheets on the bed in the corner. The Polaroid of me and Sam on my desk beside it. The succulent by the window that didn't make it to Christmas. Everything is exactly as I remember it.

Then I realize the obvious. "The gift I made you isn't here."

"Guessing that's because you haven't made it yet," Ben figures.

I can't tell if he actually believes this. Maybe he's just playing along for now. "You probably think I'm making this up."

"I didn't say that—"

"I wouldn't blame you if you did."

"It's just a lot to take in . . . Especially the boyfriend part."

"I'm sorry, he snuck up behind me," I explain. "I promise.

That's the reason I moved out. He and I broke up after my roommate—"

The door opens behind me. I hear his voice before I turn around.

"Hey, hey."

Connor comes in and throws his backpack on the bed. We haven't spoken a word since I moved out. I know he technically hasn't betrayed me yet. But it doesn't mean I have to pretend to like him. I narrow my eyes at him and say, *"You."*

He smiles at me. "What's up, Ollie?"

"Don't call me that."

His eyes widen. "Did I do something?"

"You know exactly what you did. Or what you're *going to do*."

"What am I *going* to do?"

"I know it's crossed your mind."

He looks at Ben and back at me. "I can't tell if this is a joke . . ."

He obviously has no idea what I'm talking about. But I don't owe him an explanation. I don't even want to breathe the same air. "Forget it. Let's go, Ben."

I let the door slam after we leave the room. Ben waits until we're downstairs before asking, "So what did he do exactly?"

"He's the reason I broke up with Nolan."

"I see."

Thankfully, he doesn't push for more right now. The sun is starting to fall when we're outside again. I don't even know where I'm taking us. And Julie still hasn't messaged me back. The world continues to spin around me. "I feel like I might pass out," I say out loud.

"Maybe you should rest at home."

"No, I don't want to freak out my mom."

"Then where do you want to go?"

I hadn't really considered this. I probably *should* go home. But my mom has too many things to stress about already. "I'm still figuring that out," I say breathlessly.

"You can always stay with me," Ben suggests.

I look at him. "Really?"

"I have plenty of space."

I'm surprised by his offer. Especially after everything that's transpired. I should probably say no. But I also don't want him to leave yet. "I don't want to bother you . . ."

"It wouldn't bother me," he says. "It would actually be nice to have someone to drive back with."

I think about this. It's not like I have a dorm to go back to. And Julie's date probably won't end for a while. "Okay. If you really don't mind."

Ben smiles. Then he checks the time and says, "We can head back now, if you want. I just have to remember where I parked."

It doesn't take too long to find his car. Ben opens the passenger door for me. There's an air freshener in the shape of the moon. We leave campus and turn onto the interstate.

I think everything is finally catching up to me. I feel myself drifting in and out on the way to Seattle, making the drive feel like a dream. Ben's apartment is above a convenience store. Thank god it's only two flights of stairs. It's dim when we come inside. Ben turns on a lamp in the living room.

I take a look around his apartment. It's a pretty good size for one person. There's a tiny kitchen with a kettle sitting on the stove. His refrigerator is covered with what looks like recipes.

"Do you need some water?" he asks.

The box of pastries is on the table. I feel guilty about not touching them yet, but I'm feeling exhausted all of a sudden. "I think I might just sit down for a sec," I say.

Ben shows me to the green couch in the living room. "There's supposed to be a bed in here. But it's a little finicky."

"I don't mind the sofa," I say.

"You sure? I can pull it out for you."

"No, this is good."

There's a record player on a stool by the window. If it was a different night, maybe we'd listen to some music. I would ask to see his record collection. Ben steps into his bedroom and returns with a blanket. I wasn't expecting to end up at his place tonight. Especially not for a reason like this. Ben tucks a pillow under me as I lie down. Then he heads to the kitchen and comes back with a glass of water. He sets it down and perches on the coffee table.

"I'm sorry," I say.

"About what?"

"Losing your gift."

Ben smiles. "What was it, by the way?"

"It was just a plate. But I painted stars on it."

"That would have looked nice on the coffee table."

"You probably think I'm crazy."

"I never said that," he says.

"Thanks though. For letting me stay here."

Ben hangs with me for a while, but I can barely keep my eyes open. Then he covers me with the blanket. For a second, I think he might kiss my forehead. But he just whispers, *"Goodnight, Oliver. We'll figure everything out tomorrow."*

CHAPTER TWELVE

It must have all been a weird dream because when I wake up, I'm not in Ben's apartment. I rub my eyes until everything comes into focus. The pile of clothes on the chair, the popcorn ceiling, the curtain that divides the room in half. When did I get back to my dorm? I push myself up and take a look around. I don't have to glance out the window to know it's spring again. A lawn mower passes outside, accompanied by the sound of birds.

I run my hand along the sheets, remembering the night before. Could it have really been in my head? Why do the memories feel so real? I grab my phone from the bed. There are over a dozen messages from Ben. I open them right away.

Did you leave?

> Oliver???
>
> Where did you go?
>
> Is everything ok?

I'm momentarily confused. Then I read the rest of the messages and realize—I really *was* at his apartment last night. So it wasn't a dream after all. But how did I wake up back here? I'm about to respond when I decide to call him instead. Strangely, the call doesn't go through. It doesn't even ring or go to voicemail. I send him a text message.

> Hey! sorry
>
> I'm in my dorm right now

He must be waiting by the phone. Because he responds instantly.

> Back in Ellensburg?
>
> When did you leave? I was worried about you

I wish I had an answer to this.

> I don't really remember. I just woke up here
>
> I tried calling a dozen times
>
> I just tried calling you too! It didn't go through

> Must be one of our phones

> But I'm glad to know you're safe

> One more hour and I was about to call a search team

> Sorry for scaring you. I honestly have no idea how I got back here

> I don't even remember leaving your apartment

My head is spinning again. At least everything seems back to normal. Even Ben's gift is sitting on the table. Then what exactly happened yesterday? Did I actually return to the fall? Then I remember something. Julie was supposed to call me back. I check my notifications. There are a few messages from her, too.

> Nyhavn was beautiful

> There were cute boys everywhere

> You would have loved it

The texts are followed by pictures of the waterfront. That means she's in Copenhagen. But we just saw each other yesterday. I pull up her location, which shows her thousands of miles away. I don't even know what time it is there, but I call her immediately. *She better not ignore me again.* Thankfully, she answers this time.

"*Julie!* Hello?"

There's noise in the background. "Sorry, can you hear me?"

"Yes. Where are you?"

"I'm out with some friends right now."

"So you're *not* in Ellensburg?"

"What are you talking about? Of course not."

"What about yesterday? Do you remember seeing me?"

"Seeing you *where*?"

"On campus! Outside of the library. I introduced you to Ben."

"I don't really understand the joke. But I can barely hear you." Someone is speaking to her in the background. It sounds like she's at a bar.

She doesn't remember, then. Does that mean it never happened? I have to ask one more time. "So you *really* weren't here yesterday?"

"*No*. Is everything alright?"

I'm not really sure how to answer that. I think about telling her everything, but I probably shouldn't freak her out right now. Especially while she's out with her friends. I let out a sigh and say, "Yeah, it's fine. I'll tell you about it later."

"Alright. Text me later, okay? Love you."

"Love you, too."

I say goodbye and hang up the phone. Then I check the date. I've never been so relieved to see the month of April on the screen. I even check a few news articles. A question occurs to me. I send Ben another message.

> What day is it for you?

> November third

> It's April again

> Are you sure?

> Yes, I'm looking at my calendar now

I even tell him about my call with Julie. How she's still in Copenhagen, that she doesn't remember seeing us. Neither of us can make any sense of it. There's no way Ben and I are living six months apart. How could we have seen each other yesterday?

> This is a lot to process

> You're telling me

At least we're experiencing this together, so we have each other to talk to about it with. Who else would believe any of this? A million questions run through my mind.

> I have to meet someone in the lab soon

> But let's talk later?

> No worries

I check the time again. I guess I have my own work to get started on. How am I supposed to focus on anything right now? I lie in bed for a moment longer. Then I get dressed and step outside for the first time. The spring air feels warm against my skin. Cherry blossom petals cover the ground as I make my way through campus. It's like I've woken up from a strange dream.

Then I touch my lips, remembering the kiss with Nolan. I can't believe that actually happened. He was always romantic in that way—sneaking up behind me while I was waiting in line at the dining hall, or surprising me with flowers after class. Admittedly, there are things I miss about him. But that version of him doesn't exist anymore.

I wander around campus to clear my mind. If only Ben didn't live so far away. We could meet up and talk this through in person. Hopefully, it won't be long until we see each other again . . .

It's a strange few days, sitting at the library, trying to focus on schoolwork. I wake up wondering what month it is. At least I have some structure on the weekdays. I head into my history class on Monday morning and find a seat in the back. It's another long lecture with slides slowly changing behind the professor. But it's hard to pay attention to any of it. All I can think about is Ben.

My mind goes back to Twede's Cafe. I could have sworn the door was locked when I arrived, but it somehow opened easily for Ben. And the time we met at the movie theater, I couldn't find him sitting anywhere the first time I looked around. Then I checked again and there he was. I should have known something weird was happening between us. I wonder if he's connected these things, too.

Eventually, the class ends. I wish I could go back to my dorm, but I'm scheduled to work at the library this afternoon. Unfortunately, Rami called out sick, so it's only me at the circulation desk. At least it's not too busy today. Ben hasn't texted me yet. He's probably still in class.

After checking books in and out for a few hours, I find a table to sit down at. I have several assignments I'm behind on. I pull out *The Poetics of Space* from my bag. It's been a few days since I looked at it, so I open it up to a random page and choose a passage.

"If a poet looks through a microscope or telescope, he always sees the same thing."

I'm not really sure what that means. How could you possibly see the same thing?

Sometimes it feels like I need a microscope to read between the lines in this book. If there are no wrong interpretations, it could literally mean anything at all.

And, of course, the telescope makes me think of Ben. That's probably why it caught my eye in the first place. I remember something he said to me on the roof, about the universe. *The more we find out, the more we realize how little we actually know about it.*

I read the passage over again. Maybe it's about the process of searching itself. Both the microscope and the telescope allow us to gaze into the unknown, hoping to find something meaningful—a discovery that only leads to a million more possibilities. I grab a pencil and start writing down every thought that comes to me.

* * *

The rest of the school day is uneventful. I'm just counting down the hours until I hear from Ben. He's been extra busy with classes this week. It's not until I'm back in my dorm that I get a text from him.

> Sorry for taking so long

> Just getting home now

> Any new developments on your end?

> Not as far as I know

> I wish we could call each other

> Yeah me too

I try his number again. But it still doesn't go through.

> Have you told anyone else about it?

> No not yet

> I barely believe any of it myself

> I know what you mean. I haven't either

I considered telling Julie everything. But she might think I'm playing some prank on her, which wouldn't be completely out of character for me. I'll decide this later.

> I didn't get the chance to say this before, but I had a lot of fun with you last time

> Sorry this might have ruined it

< It didn't ruin anything

< I had a great time too

> Thanks again for letting me stay over

< Anytime

< Sad I didn't get the chance to make you breakfast though

I smile at his message.

> Raincheck for next time?

< Definitely

< I can't wait to see you again

I'm so glad this hasn't scared him off. We text for a while longer, making plans to meet up again. I'm not sure how we're going to find each other, but somehow it's worked so far. Maybe we can figure it out in person.

> Can I ask you one more thing

> Do you really believe all of this?
>
> It's okay if you don't

He doesn't take long to respond.

> I'm not really sure what's going on
>
> But I trust you

> Thank you

I keep the phone close to me as I lie in bed. This feels like some strange dream. But I'm glad I don't have to experience it alone.

CHAPTER THIRTEEN

It's a Saturday afternoon in downtown Seattle. I'm supposed to meet Ben at the entrance of the street fair. He's with his little cousin who's visiting from Colorado. He promised to watch her for a few hours. It's been a full week since we've seen each other. I was hoping to come yesterday, but Mom came down with the flu. She called me to pick up some medicine from the pharmacy. Thankfully, she didn't have a fever or anything. I checked in on her before I left this morning.

I'm a little nervous about seeing Ben today. How did we find each other the last few times? The street fair should be taking place right now. I'm hoping to find a line of tents as I turn the corner, but the sidewalks are completely empty. I was worried this would happen when I arrived.

> I think I'm here

> But I don't see anything

> Which tent are you standing at?

> There are no tents...

> oh

> You're at the right place?

> I just put in the address you sent

> But there's nothing here

> What are you next to?

I take a look around me.

> There's a giant mural of a mountain

> Okay I know where that is

> Just stay there and I'll come find you

Several minutes go by. I keep looking around, watching the cars pass along the road. Then I check the date on my phone again. *April 16th*. The street fair probably happened months ago. I know Ben said to wait here, but what if I am at the wrong location? I take a step and suddenly a breeze pushes against my back, accompanied by music from a speaker behind me.

I turn around and everything has changed. The street is suddenly filled with people. Lights glow above the tents that line the block, and smoke billows from the grills behind them. Then I hear my name through the crowd.

"Oliver! There you are—"

Ben smiles as he makes his way over. The next thing I know, my arms wrap tightly around him. Ben squeezes me back and whispers, *"I was a little worried there."*

"Glad you found me," I say.

"Told you I would."

Cold air blows through my hair. Thankfully, I brought a jacket this time. I'm still not sure how I found myself back here, but all that matters is we're together again. We smile at each other. Then a girl appears from behind him. She's wearing a Hello Kitty puffer coat. Ben puts a hand on her shoulder and says, "This is Leah. We're hanging out today."

I crouch down a little. "Nice to meet you, Leah. I love your crown." It's a plastic tiara with pink flowers.

She just smiles at me.

"It's her birthday tomorrow," Ben says.

"Well, happy birthday! Soon you'll be old enough to gamble."

Ben chuckles. "She's a little shy."

"Oh, I don't bite. Right, Ben?" I wink at him. Then I straighten up and take a look around. "What have you two been up to so far?"

"We did a little exploring," Ben says. "But we haven't been here very long. Leah wants a something to eat."

I smile. "So what are we standing around for?"

Ben takes Leah by the hand, and we make our way through the maze of tents. There must be a thousand people here. It's hard to believe the street was empty a minute ago.

Along the way, we stop by a table of handmade cards. I

think about buying a pink one for Julie. I know how much she loves handwritten notes. At the food tents there's a cute stand selling Korean street food. The potato corn dogs look especially good. We order three of them, along with some grilled tteokbokki and fries.

"I got this one," Ben insists.

"Okay, I'll get us dessert."

Since I'm holding the tteokbokki, Ben puts a fry into my mouth.

"No ketchup?" I ask.

We laugh as we continue through the fair. There's a tent giving out free ice cream samples. Surprisingly, our favorite flavor is Olive Oil Cheesecake. I offer to buy something for Leah. "Do you want a strawberry-colored cone? The pink will go nicely with your crown."

"Mom said I can't have more sweets," she says.

I lean down and whisper, "But she's not here, is she?"

Ben gives me a look. *Oliver . . .*

"She deserves one. It's her birthday tomorrow." I wink at her.

"Alright," he agrees. Then he turns to Leah. "But don't tell your mom."

I get Leah a scoop of vanilla with sprinkles. This must change her mind about me, because she takes my hand instead of Ben's.

There are a few carnival-style games farther down. Ring toss, balloon darts, the infamous duck pond. I haven't played any of these in a long time. Ben gestures at the wall of prizes. "Leah was eyeing the stuffed animals earlier. I told her we'd come back to look at them."

"Which one?" I ask her.

YOU'VE FOUND OLIVER

"The blue panda," she says.

I squeeze her hand. "Well, let's get him."

We walk up to the tent where three bottles are stacked on a circular stand. The rules are pretty simple: You have to knock them completely off the stand to win. The guy behind the counter places a pile of beanbags in front of us. I look at Ben and say, "Wanna see who can knock down the most?"

He smiles. "Only if we make it interesting."

"Go on . . ."

"What if the winner gets a special prize?"

"And what should that be?"

"Good question." He rubs his chin. "I have to think about it."

"How about the winner decides later," I suggest.

"I like that idea."

I offer to go first. I don't tell Ben that I'm an expert at this. It's one of the games our school always had at spring festival. I used to have fun beating Sam all the time. Of course, I have to play it cool. I don't want to go too hard on the first throw. I toss the beanbag, knocking two bottles off the stand.

Ben smiles. "That was pretty good."

"Just warming up."

He stretches his arm before throwing the beanbag, hard, and knocking all the bottles off the stand.

"Where did you learn to aim like that?"

"Varsity tennis," he says casually.

How did I forget about that? I read his bio in the article I found online. I should have guessed he had a competitive side. He runs a hand through his hair and winks at me. But I don't let this intimidate me—because I have a competitive side, too. I crack my knuckles and pick up another beanbag.

My eyes focus on the center of the bottles. I throw harder this time, knocking them all over.

"An improvement." Ben nods respectfully. Then he picks up another beanbag. His first throw clearly wasn't beginner's luck, because he knocks off all the bottles a second time. This kicks me into Super Saiyan mode and I deliver another perfect throw, but Ben does it again, and again. This goes on for several more rounds, each of us missing a few here and there until I ultimately win by a single point.

Ben shakes my hand and says, "Good game. Didn't realize I was up against a world champion."

"Headed to the Olympics next year."

"Glad you're representing our country."

We win enough times to get the extra-large blue panda. It's twice the size of Leah. I have to carry it for her as we continue down the street. We buy some chocolate bars from one of the tents, and then Leah wants to go on the kiddie rides. She picks the bumper cars, and we wait by the railing.

"Sorry you have to babysit with me," Ben says.

I shrug. "What do you mean? I'm having a good time."

Ben smiles. "Good. We can do something after, too. I'll have to take her home soon. Unless you have other plans."

"I may have to meet some other friends." I pretend to check my phone. "Oh, they just cancelled. Guess that means I'm completely free."

"You're cute," he says, smirking. "Have you decided what you prize you want?"

"I'm still thinking about it . . ."

"Take your time." He unwraps his chocolate bar and takes a bite. Then he holds it out to me and says, "Wanna try?"

"Sure."

I lean forward and take a small bite. There's caramel inside. I must have gotten some on my face, because Ben wipes it off with his thumb. We look at each other for a moment. Then we turn to the bumper cars. Competitiveness must run in their family. Leah is unforgiving as she bumps into the other kids, regardless of their age. I cheer her on.

"Good aim, Leah! Take him out, too!"

We leave the fair around sunset to take Leah back to her hotel. Ben carries her on his shoulders the whole way there. It's sweet, the way he takes care of her. I'm reminded that he once had a sibling, too. I let him say goodbye before we head off on our own.

"Should we hang at my place?"

"Lead the way."

CHAPTER FOURTEEN

"Wanna listen to some music?"

Ben lights a candle on the coffee table and lifts the lid of the record player. The place is smaller than I remember. There's a fire escape directly outside the window that's cracked open. I stare at the laundromat across the street and say, "I didn't notice the view before."

"Yeah, it's not much to look at."

"I'd take this over a roommate any day."

"For sure." Ben opens the drawer beneath the television, revealing a modest record collection. "There's no one to complain about my music taste. Except for the woman upstairs occasionally. Are you feeling something upbeat or moody?"

"Have anything from the Velvet Underground?"

Ben smiles. "Unfortunately, no. But I have Joni Mitchell."

"Ooh, which album?"

"*Court and Spark.*" He holds up the cover to show me.

"I don't think I've heard that one."

"Allow me to indoctrinate you." Ben moves the needle and puts the record on the turntable. "This thing can be a little wonky." He hits the side of the record player. The sound of a piano slowly fills the apartment. "There we go." Ben turns around and smiles warmly. Then he grabs the bag of snacks we picked up earlier and hands me my drink.

"Thanks." I open the can and take a sip. Then I take another look around the room. I didn't notice all the Polaroids on the wall last time. Probably because I was half asleep. I walk around the sofa to get a closer look. There are dozens of them that must have been taken over the years. It reminds me of the one I keep of me and Sam. I find a funny one of Ben holding his tennis racket to his face. He's looking through it like a chain-link fence. I stare at it and say, "When did you stop playing tennis again? You definitely still have the muscle for it."

"You think so?" Ben flexes his right arm.

"Stop showing off."

He laughs. Then he comes over to see which photo I'm looking at. "I honestly miss it sometimes. It was hard to juggle with school and everything. Maybe I'd have a better social life if I managed both. But I probably wouldn't have time to sleep. You're actually my first guest here. Besides my parents, of course."

"I'm honored."

"Actually—"

Ben disappears into the bedroom for a second. Then he comes out with a camera. "I was planning on making this a tradition. You can be the first guest photo on the wall." He turns the camera on and holds it eye level. "Are you ready?"

"What should I do?"

"Just act natural."

"Okay. But make sure it's cute."

"You always look cute," he assures me.

Of course, this makes me smile. Ben takes a picture of me sitting on the sofa, pretending to read a magazine. The Polaroid immediately prints from the camera. Ben hands it to me and says, "It takes a few minutes to develop."

"You don't have to shake it?"

"That actually ruins the photo."

I gasp. "They've been lying to us?"

Ben lets me pick my spot on the wall. "Perfect," he says, and tapes it down.

We step back together, taking another look at the wall. It really adds life to the apartment. "How long have you had the camera?"

"It belonged to my brother," Ben says. "He had it for as long as I can remember. It's just been sitting in his room since he died, so I decided to take it with me."

"Do you have a picture of him?"

"Yeah." Ben points to another photo. "That's him there."

I lean forward to see better. It's a picture of them together as kids. They're standing in a kitchen wearing matching blue sweaters. His brother's arm is around Ben's shoulders.

"His name was Peter," Ben says.

"You told me before. He sort of looks like you."

"I don't have a lot of photos of us, to be honest."

"Well, this is one is perfect," I say.

Joni Mitchell's voice continues to fill the apartment. Ben pours the snacks onto the table for us to share. Then we sit on the couch together, enjoying the music. He knows practically all of the lyrics, repeating them to me like lines of poetry. It's a pretty short album. So we put on *Clouds* next, which is my personal favorite. But I'm more focused on how close we're sitting, the way our legs and shoulders touch occasionally. The way our eyes meet when he turns his head. When the conversation quiets, I finally decide to ask, "How come I haven't seen your room yet?"

"That's a good question."

I smile as he rises to his feet. Then he holds out a hand and pulls me up as well. It's dark when we enter the bedroom. Ben turns on a desk lamp, casting the room in a soft pink glow. It's a small room, large enough for a full-size bed and a single nightstand. There's not a lot of décor, except a few baseball hats hanging on the wall.

"It's not much to look at," Ben says.

"No, it's cozy. It's giving—" I pause to think of the right words. "Straight-college-guy minimal chic."

"I'll take that, I guess."

At least there's a small window in here. "Do you get a lot of light in the morning?"

"Not really. But I sit on the fire escape sometimes."

I glance at the time on my phone. I'm not sure when the last bus leaves tonight. At one point, the music ends. Ben heads out to replace the record. My thoughts run together—he hasn't told me to leave yet. . . . Does he want to go back to the living room? . . . Is he waiting for me to make a decision? Eventually, I sit down on his bed and lean back a little. Ben returns to the room. He looks at me for a moment, then sits beside me.

The music pours through the doorway. I like how soft the

lamplight is here. Especially the way it hits his skin. The definition of Ben's shoulders really comes through in his white T-shirt. He looks at me and says, "How do you feel about this album? Because I can change it to something else."

"I like it. Let's enjoy it from right here."

We both lie down and stare at the ceiling as the next song comes on. Then we turn to face each other.

"Is it okay if I stay over again?"

"I was already assuming you would," he says, looking at me. "But you don't have to sleep on the couch if you don't want to."

"I didn't mind it. But the bed is more comfortable."

Ben smiles. "You know, you never told me what the winner gets."

I almost forgot about that. "I'm still deciding."

"You're really taking your time."

"I mean, what's the rush?"

Ben stares at me, eyes shining. Then he runs a hand through my hair. "I didn't say this earlier, but I was worried I might not see you again. I don't know what I would have done if that happened. This whole thing is so weird, right?"

"If I'm being honest, I'm surprised you haven't run off yet," I admit. "Even I'm having trouble believing it."

"I'm here till the bitter end." He touches my nose playfully. "Even if you are making this all up."

"That would be a funny way to get your attention."

"It really would, considering you already had it." He smiles again. "Why else would I have skipped lab and driven two hours to see you?"

"That would be silly."

"There is something else though. Something that makes

me believe all this."

"What is it?"

"That first night we met at the diner, when we couldn't find each other." He pauses for a moment. "I was standing outside and then you appeared out of nowhere. I thought I was crazy for a second. I guess it all makes sense now."

The past two weeks replay in my head. "At the very least, I hear trauma bonding really connects people."

Ben brushes his finger across my cheek. "I think we've both gone through more traumatic things. This is just something we can't explain right now."

"Like a lot of things in the universe, right?"

"Exactly." Then he glances at my bracelet. "Where did you get this from?"

I always forget I'm wearing it. "Oh. Sam gave it to me."

He touches it. "I like it. Do you still have a lot of his stuff?"

"I wouldn't say a lot. But a few things."

He's quiet for a moment, like he's thinking about something. "Can I ask you another question about him? I'm not sure if it's too personal." He waits for a nod from me to continue. "Were you two ever more than friends?"

"What makes you ask that?"

"When you were still texting Sam, you said that you loved him."

This catches me off guard. I keep forgetting about all those messages. "We were best friends. I told you that."

"Did you want it to be more?"

I feel like he already knows the answer. "Maybe. It doesn't really matter anymore." I never thought I'd admit that to anyone. But it doesn't feel like Ben is judging me. I feel like I can trust him. "We did kiss once though. Only once. It happened a long time ago. I've never told anyone. Not even Julie."

"Do you think it would bother her?"

"I don't think so. It happened before they met. She knows we'd been friends forever. And I've told her a lot of other things. I think I'm allowed to have one secret." *Maybe she even has one, too,* I think.

Ben nods. "That's fair."

"What about you? Do you have any secrets?"

He takes a moment. "Ask me again later."

"Okay. I will."

The song changes from the living room. Ben takes my hand, intertwining our fingers. "Let me know if you're tired," he says.

"I'm wide awake."

He smiles. "I'm glad you came over."

"Me too. Hopefully, I won't disappear on you again."

"Don't worry. I'm not taking my eyes off you this time."

"If you keep staring at me like that, I might just get stuck here."

"Would that be so bad?"

I think about it. "Not necessarily. I mean, it's only six months, right? I wouldn't mind redoing a few things. Maybe bring my grades up."

"That's the first I've heard you talk about grades."

"*Hey.*" I push him playfully. "We can't all be perfect."

"Is that a nice way of calling me a nerd?"

We smile at each other. In the living room, the song "Both Sides Now" is playing. Ben turns his ear toward it and says, "My favorite song of hers."

"Mine too."

I'm not sure if that was true before. But it will be now.

I stare into his deep brown eyes. I'm not going to miss my chance this time. I hope he's thinking the same thing I am.

"*Ben*," I whisper.

"Yeah?"

"I think I've decided what the winner gets."

He waits for me to continue. But I don't say anything else. I just lean forward until I feel his lips against mine. A rush of warmth passes between us. Like sunlight on skin.

We fall asleep in each other's arms.

CHAPTER FIFTEEN

"Did you forget about me?"

Petals fall from the sky as I slowly open my eyes. But I don't have to look to know whose voice that is. I would recognize his voice anywhere. I turn my head anyway. Sam is lying in the grass beside me, waiting for a response. We stare at each other for a moment. When I don't answer, he repeats the question.

"I said, did you forget about me?"

"Of course not," I say finally. "How could you ask that?"

"Because I haven't seen you lately. And I've missed you."

"I missed you, too." *You know I do.*

Sam smiles as petals continue to fall. He puts his arms behind his head and looks up at the sky. "It's been a while since we've been out here, huh?"

I push myself up with one arm, taking in the view around us. We're lying out by the lake again, surrounded by flowers.

It's only the two of us out here.

Eventually, Sam looks at me again. "Remember when we snuck out of school to go for a swim?"

"Which time?"

"The first one. You got us in so much trouble."

"Me? It was *your* idea."

Sam laughs, facing the sky again. "Maybe you're right. My memory's a little fuzzy. I really miss those days though. I miss a lot of things. Do you still come here a lot?"

"Not as much as before."

"Why not?"

"Because you're not here anymore . . ."

"That's not true," he says. "I'll always be here."

I don't say anything else back. I just take in this moment we have together. It feels like old times again. Part of me knows this is a dream. But I don't want it to end yet. So I lie back down and stare at the clouds with him.

Sam turns his head. "So you really miss me?"

It's just like him to keep asking. "More than you could know, Sam."

He smiles at me and stares out at the water. Then he asks, "Wasn't there something you wanted to tell me?"

At first, I'm not sure what he's talking about. Then I remember the last time we saw each other. We stood near the cliff during the night of the bonfire. I was about to tell him that I loved him. But he left before I got the chance. Sometimes, I wonder what would have happened if he stayed a moment longer. Maybe he would still be alive.

"I don't know if that matters anymore," I answer.

"How come?"

"Because it's too late now."

A strong wind rolls through us, ruffling the leaves above us. Then the clouds begin to darken, casting shadows along the water. "Looks like we'll have to leave soon," Sam says. "But I want to show you something first . . ."

Sam rises to his feet, and heads for the trees. I get up to follow after him.

"Sam, wait—"

I have no idea where he's leading me. I just follow along, taking careful steps as we move through the trees. The light is fading faster than usual. By the time we break through the other side, it's completely dark out. The mist fades, revealing a field of grass that stretches toward a night sky. It takes me a few seconds to realize where we are. We're standing at the city limit, where Ellensburg is set apart from the rest of the world.

Every now and then, Sam and I would walk out here. Mostly when we were tired of school, home, and everything else. We would stand at this very line, talking about our plans to leave someday. Then we would cross over it together. I watch as Sam steps toward the line, pausing just short of it. He stares down at the grass and back at me. Then he slowly raises his foot into the air as if to take a big step forward.

But he doesn't, he just lowers his foot back down. "Guess this is as far as I can go, huh?" Then he looks at me, eyes twinkling. "But you can still leave."

I stare down at my shoes, unsure this time. I can feel him watching me. I know he's waiting for me to try it next. So I step forward, crossing the line without him. The temperature drops a little, sending a slight chill through me.

"There you go." Sam stands there with his hands in his pockets. Then he smiles and says, "You'll have to let me know what's on the other side."

I don't say anything. I look ahead, staring out at the field of grass, taking in the line of mountains in the distance, the moon hanging over it. When I finally turn back around, Sam is gone.

Just like that.

I'm alone again.

What if I don't want to go any farther? What if I want everything back the way it was?

I used to dream about him all the time. Particularly on the nights I felt most alone. I would close my eyes and find him waiting for me again. Some of them feel more real than others, especially ones like this. Part of me thinks it's really him in the dream. Maybe it's a place we can meet between our worlds. Or maybe it's just my imagination and I'm sitting by myself at the lake. But the dreams are happening less these days. I'm not ready to lose him yet.

CHAPTER SIXTEEN

I wake up in my dorm again. I lie there for a moment, allowing the room to come into focus. How did I get back here? I remember falling asleep in Ben's bed, our arms wrapped around each other. I wonder if he's noticed I'm gone yet. I hate that I keep disappearing on him. Especially after such a special night. I can still feel his lips pressed against mine. Then I look around for my phone. There's a message from him.

> Where did you disappear to again?

> Please text me when you get this

I respond right away.

> Hey!

> Sorry
>
> I woke up in Ellensburg again
>
> But I'm okay!

He responds a few seconds later.

> I was waiting to hear from you
>
> Glad you're okay

> I don't know how that keeps happening

> So you don't remember leaving?

> Not at all! I honestly have no clue how I got back
>
> I just woke up in my bed again

> It seems like this always happens after you fall asleep

> That's so weird

> yeah I know
>
> At least we got to spend some time together

I take a deep breath and let it out. Maybe we should focus on the good.

> Thanks for letting me stay over again

> I had a great night

Me too

But I was hoping you'd stay longer this time

Was planning to cook French toast for breakfast this morning. Had all the ingredients and everything

> Ugh that sounds really good

> Sorry to disappoint you

> Hopefully it won't always be this way

Its ok

Will save it for another day

I hadn't truly considered this. The thought of never being able to wake up with him. See his face in the morning light. Sit down and have breakfast together. Are those things we'll never get to share? I remember thinking how hard a long-distance relationship would be. Now we've found ourselves in different timelines. I still can't wrap my head around any of this.

But I'm missing you already

> I miss you too

I lie down and hold the phone close to me. Maybe it doesn't matter how or why this is happening. There's a world out there where we're still strangers. I'm just happy we found each other in this strange glitch in the universe. All that matters is Ben and I have each other. Even if it's only momentary.

Flowers are blooming outside. You become more aware of the seasons when you're moving between them. I imagine leaves falling wherever Ben is right now. It's an odd feeling, walking through the same world, experiencing something different. Does that mean there's another version of him here, doing something else? Would he even know who I am? I think about this as I head to the library. Thankfully, Rami is back this week. We spend the first hour catching up on everything.

"How was your trip?" I ask him.

Rami sips his coffee and says, "Honestly, exhausting. We were craving Mexican food but couldn't find anything good. But what do you expect from *Canada*?" He was in Vancouver for the weekend with the chess club. "My friend Maki had a great time though. Except the part where he got robbed. There are pickpockets everywhere these days."

"Oh god, what did they take?"

Rami waves it off. "Don't worry, he's broke. And I'm honestly glad he lost that hideous thing he called a bag. Must have had five dollars in there at most, which he owed *me*.

Should have taken his shirt while they were at it. Who still wears tie-dye these days?" Rami pretends to shiver at the thought. "Anyway, enough about that. What about you? Are you still talking to that Ben guy?"

"Of course I am. I stayed at his place last night."

"Oh. Does that mean it's serious?"

"I don't know about *serious*. But we definitely like each other a lot."

"Then why aren't you exclusive? Hasn't it been a month now?"

I lean back in the chair and say, "It's complicated. I mean, he lives over a hundred miles away." Obviously, I don't tell him the other reason.

"Hmm. So he wants to be open," Rami assumes.

"That's not what I said! The distance is just"—I pause, wondering how to phrase this—"*more than I thought*, okay?"

Rami nods. "That can be a deal-breaker for most people. I don't know of any long-distance relationship that's actually worked—"

I hold up a hand. "That's not why I told you, Rami. You're supposed to reassure me that everything is going to be okay."

"Oh, *right*," he corrects himself. "What I *meant* to say was that some distance could be good for you. Look at John and Savannah."

"Who are John and Savannah?"

"From *Dear John*?" He rolls his eyes as if I should know that. "It's such a good movie. He goes off to war for two years and they never stop sending each other letters."

"What happens in the end?"

"It's actually been a while since I've seen it," he says, scratching his head. "I think he dies of cancer and she marries someone else . . . You know what, maybe I'm thinking of *The Notebook*. Or do they both die in that, too?"

"Rami, those are terrible examples."

He frowns. "Sorry. I'm dyslexic."

"What does that have to do with anything?"

I decide to end the conversation there. At least his heart is in the right place. The library is starting to get busy anyway. Rami and I have to get back to work. Of course, I don't stop thinking about Ben. I know things will work out for us.

It's another long week of classes. But I can't seem to focus on anything. I just stare out the windows, wondering when we'll see each other again. I wish I could just hop on the next bus to Seattle. But I'm falling behind on my schoolwork, which includes a history paper I haven't even started yet. And I just got an email about fall classes; registration is opening up soon. I haven't even finished this quarter yet. How am I supposed to know what to take next year?

I wish I didn't have to think about this right now. I'm still trying to figure out what's been happening between me and Ben. I've started searching online for similar stories. Forums or articles that might explain how our timelines seem to have crossed. I haven't found anything helpful, just sci-fi references. There's one movie, *Sliding Doors*, that I've watched with my mom. It's about a woman who nearly misses the train, creating two versions of herself: one where she gets on the train and another where she misses it.

I wonder if things like this happen all the time. The decisions we make create alternate timelines with different versions of ourselves. Of course, that's just a movie, but maybe something I did connected me to Ben. There has to be an answer out there somewhere.

Thankfully, the week always ends with Professor Clarke's class. It's the only class I never consider skipping. And it's not just because she's Julie's mom. There's another quote on the board when I walk into the room.

"Memories are motionless, and the more securely they are fixed in space, the sounder they are." —Gaston Bachelard

For some reason, the desks are arranged differently today. They're spread out in no particular order. Professor Clarke must notice our confusion. "You may take a seat anywhere," she says. "Feel free to move the desks around or sit on the floor, if you'd like. Or you could stand. I won't stop you."

I take a seat somewhere in the middle of the room. Usually, Professor Clarke teaches at the front of the classroom. But today, she is standing by the opened windows, forcing some of us to turn our chairs around.

"You're probably wondering why we're sitting this way today," she continues. "My question back to you would be, why did you sit the way you were before? After all, I never gave assigned seating in this class. I also never said you couldn't move things around. You simply walked in and sat down in the same spot every day." She points at someone standing by the corner. "Ryan, why did you choose to stand today?"

He shrugs. "Been sitting all day. My legs are kinda sore."

"I imagine that happens a lot."

"Yeah, I guess."

"You never thought to stand before?"

He shakes his head. "No."

Professor Clarke points to someone else. "Sierra, why

have you never moved your desk around?"

"I don't know," she says timidly. "I didn't really think about it."

Professor Clarke takes this in and says, "I'm sure this seems insignificant. The way we arrange ourselves in a classroom. But this course is about questioning *everything*, which includes things you never once thought to question. Let's keep this in mind as we move on to today's discussion."

She steps toward the chalkboard. "*Memories are motionless . . .*" As usual, she lets the words sink in. "Some of you have encountered this passage in the text already. Admittedly, this is a bit of a tricky one, so I thought we might use this time to read between the lines together.

"According to Bachelard, memories are fixed to the locations in which they are made, like the homes we've previously discussed. Just like a scent can conjure a memory, so can a particular hallway or room when you walk through it. Have you ever forgotten something only to have it all come flooding back to you when you glance at a photograph? Every room, in every building, including this one, has memories of its own. Ones that have existed since long before any you, or myself, stepped foot in here," she says.

"That is one way for us to interpret his use of *motionless*. Memories are anchored in space. However, when it comes to time, our sense of memory is never fixed." Her eyes scan the room. "After all, you can't imagine time the same way you can visualize a room, can you? What would that look like if you tried? The moving hands of a clock? Images passing through a film reel? We all experience it differently. That's because time is never constant, but always in *motion*.

"Think about that for a moment. Why do certain things

that happened years ago feel like yesterday? Why do some days feel longer than others? How do we recall some memories instantly, regardless of when they happened? If the past is constantly merging with present, maybe time shouldn't be represented on a single line, as we often regard it. Maybe time is an infinite number of lines that we can access at any moment, likes stars in the sky."

Professor Clarke picks up a piece of chalk from the board. "We've been working as a class these past few weeks. For today's activity, we're going to do something different. I would like you to write about a memory from your life. You will not be turning this in to me. This is something I want you to write for yourself. Think back to the corners of the room where you sat alone. After all, it's the moments of solitude when we can access our full imagination."

She writes down a few more things on the board. Then she hands out blank paper. A few people move their desks to the windows. I take out a pen and think about what to write. My mind goes back to the home, since that's what we've been focusing on. *Memories are anchored in space.* Maybe that's why I struggle with these assignments. Because I've blocked so much out. But a home can be made anywhere, right? Like the places I've known all my life. I have memories attached to every inch of Ellensburg. Of course, a lot of these were with Sam. The two of us sitting by the lake together. Watching the sunset on our walk home. Riding our bikes around the neighborhood.

Maybe that's why I don't want to move away. Because I can still feel his presence everywhere. I don't remember what I had for breakfast yesterday, but I remember what movie we watched on his couch when we were snowed in that winter.

Or the time he carried me on his back when I hurt my knee playing soccer. Whatever broken home I inhabited, at least he was a part of it. He was always there for me. The only place left to see him is in my dreams. But I keep waking up from them.

Maybe if I went back more than six months—maybe I could have saved you.

I continue writing until the end of class. Then I tuck the paper into my bag and head out.

It's raining a little tonight. Mom texted me a few hours ago, asking if I wanted to come home for dinner. She's been sick for almost a week now but seems to be feeling a lot better today.

We make orange chicken and broccoli, which I might have slightly burned. Mom says it gives it a "nice char." At least the rice is cooked perfectly. Of course, she serves the food on the ceramic plate we made. She's been wanting to take another pottery class together.

"I can look into it tomorrow," I say.

"Are your classes going well?"

"They're fine. Just a lot of catching up to do." I take a bite.

"And how was your trip to Seattle? I've been meaning to ask you."

"It was fun," I say casually. "They had this really big street fair. You know, played some games, had some corn dogs."

"Which friends did you go with?"

"His name is Ben."

"Ben . . ." She repeats his name. "Don't know if you've

mentioned him before."

I take another bite. "He actually lives in Seattle. I was visiting him."

"How do you two know each other?"

"He's a new friend. But we've been chatting for a while."

"It's quite the commute to meet someone, don't you think?"

"It's not the first time we met," I explain. "He's visited me, too. I showed him around Ellensburg. He goes to the University of Washington. He's a first year like I am. He studies astronomy."

"Well, that's a very good school."

"Yeah, he's really smart," I tell her. "He's really into space and stuff. For his graduation gift, he picked out a telescope. Isn't that funny?"

Mom nods with approval. "Sounds like a refined young man. Hopefully, I'll get to meet him one day."

"Yeah. Hopefully."

I don't say anything else because I'm realizing that might never happen: the two of them being in the same room together. The thought of this breaks my heart a little. So I push it out of my mind.

At least Ben and I can see each other. For now, that's all that matters to me.

CHAPTER SEVENTEEN

I wake up early to call Julie. She's been traveling around Northern Europe for the past few days, sending me photos of her trip. We haven't had the chance to talk over the phone. She should have returned to Copenhagen this morning. I've been waiting all week to catch up with her.

It always takes ages for her to answer. *Will you pick up already.*

"Julie? Are you there—"

"Sorry, I literally just got home," she says finally. "Long day again. We went to this gorgeous harbor bath. I'll send you a photo of it. Apparently, everyone's into cold plunging here. I didn't do it, obviously. But it was interesting to watch."

"Honestly, that sounds nice right about now."

"It's supposed to be good for your health. I really wish you could visit. I miss you."

"I miss you, too."

"What have you been up to? Tell me everything."

"Oh, you know . . . school, work, Ben."

"Right, the new boy. How are things going with him?"

It feels strange keeping things a secret from her. I wonder if I should just tell her already. "The distance is still a lot. But we're making it work so far."

"That's good to hear. Are you seeing each other again this weekend?"

I sigh. "I wish. He has this research presentation. He's been stressing about it all day. We're making plans to see each other next week though."

"What kind of research does he do?" she asks.

"He's an astronomy major. So something smart like that."

"Why don't you go to his presentation and surprise him? I bet he'd really appreciate that."

"Do you think I should?"

"It could be really sweet," Julie says. "I remember performing something at a poetry reading once. Sam was the only one who showed up. It's one of the moments that made me realize I was falling in love with him."

Sam was always thoughtful that way. Maybe I could borrow a page from his playbook. "That might not be a bad idea. Since it sounds important to him. It's not like I have other plans tonight, unless you count rewatching *Downton Abbey*."

"Oliver, you've watched every season twice already."

"That's what makes it comforting. I already know what happens."

Julie sighs. "Sounds like you need a break from your dorm. What about that Pindar Dance? Isn't that happening tonight?"

"It's next weekend."

"You should invite Ben to that."

"It's way too expensive," I remind her.

"But I thought you had tickets already?"

"Correction, they were *Nolan's* tickets. And I have a hunch he's not taking me anymore." The Pindar Dance is an annual formal that begins with a fancy four-course dinner. It was created by some rich alumni who wanted to make sure students knew the right spoon to use.

Julie exhales. "Well, forget it, then. I'm sure you'll find something better to do."

It sounds pretentious anyway, having to dress up in a suit and tie. Admittedly, it might be fun to experience that once. But it's not like I can go with Ben anyway. I guess there are a lot of things we can't do together.

I must have gone quiet for a long time, because Julie says, "Is everything else alright? I've been a little worried since our last call."

I think about how to answer this. Part of me wants to tell her everything, but how would I even explain it to her? Maybe there's a way to ease it in. "Actually, I do have a question. If I told you something crazy, would you believe me?"

"Like what?"

"If something unexplainable happened and I decided to tell you, would you believe me?"

"Is it about Sam?"

"No . . . Why?"

"I was just wondering."

"It's not about him." Well, not really.

"Then what is it?"

"It's a hypothetical question, okay? Just answer it."

There's a brief silence. Then she says, "Of course I would believe you. You can tell me anything. No matter what it is."

"I really appreciate that."

"Is there something you want to tell me?"

Another silence.

"Maybe not this second," I say.

"Well, okay. You know how to reach me."

Thankfully, she doesn't push me. This would be so much easier in person. I'm sure I'll tell her eventually. For now, we just chat like old times. It's nice hearing her voice over the phone. Julie tells me about her trip to Lund. Apparently, it's only a short train ride from Copenhagen. She went on a spontaneous date with some Swedish boy who showed her the best meatballs she's ever had. It's to be determined if they'll see each other again, which she seems to find more romantic to leave up to fate. It sounds like she's truly having a great time. I bet she would stay longer if she could.

After we hang up, I call my mom. She's working a half shift today. I ask if I can borrow the car when she's back. I think about what Julie suggested earlier. Ben's conference should go into the evening. That gives me plenty of time to get there.

* * *

Flags flutter above the entrance of the Plaza Hotel. Ben mentioned where he'd be over text this morning. I hurry into the lobby and look for the elevators. The conference room should be on the seventh floor (I checked online before I left). I thought about bringing him flowers, but I didn't want to get here too late. Especially since Ben doesn't know I'm coming.

I'm hoping I'll find a crowd of students to follow. But the elevator opens to an empty floor. I turn down the hall and manage to find the conference room. All of the doors are locked. I probably should have planned this better. How close do we need to be to find each other? I try to turn the handle one more time. It doesn't sound like anyone's on the other side. Several minutes go by. I'll have to let Ben know I'm here. I'm sure he'll still be surprised.

A man approaches from behind.

"Can I help you, sir?"

I turn around to face him. "Uh, just waiting on a friend," I say.

"Does he have a room here?"

"Maybe . . ."

"I'm gonna have to ask you to wait downstairs."

I should have lied better. "Just let me text him real quick—"

As I'm about to press *send*, the doors behind me open and a crowd begins to pour out, filling the hall with students wearing colorful lanyards. The security guard has vanished. I stand there for a second, taking in my surroundings. A sign has appeared next to the door: ASTRONOMY, ASTROPHYSICS & SCIENCE EDUCATION. So this is the right place! Ben must be somewhere nearby. I head into the conference room to look for him.

Display boards line the tables; students are presenting their research. I walk through the middle row, glancing at images of planets, quasars, and other things I don't recognize.

That's when I see him, standing by his poster, wearing a blue tie.

Ben is talking to a small group gathered near his table. It's like catching him in his natural habitat. I wonder what my equivalent would be. Probably lying in bed, scrolling through my phone. He looks so handsome in his button-up shirt, hair brushed to one side. It's worth traveling back in time just to see him like this.

I don't want to interrupt anything, so I wait at a distance until the group of students moves on, leaving him standing alone.

Then I casually walk over, using my professional voice. "Well, this poster looks *very* promising."

Ben turns his head, ready to answer questions. Then his eyes widen. "Oliver? What are you doing here?"

"I came to support you. And learn about space, of course."

Ben smiles. "How did you get in?"

I point back to the doors. "The entrance. Why, did I need a ticket or something?"

"I guess in theory," he says. "I had to apply for funding. I think a badge may be four hundred dollars."

"I guess that makes me a criminal." I hold out my wrists. "Arrest me, officer."

The people standing nearby give me a weird look. Ben pushes my hands down and whispers, "I'm sure you're in the clear." Then he smiles wider. "I can't believe you came all the way here. I wasn't expecting to see anyone."

"Thought I would surprise you."

"That's sweet of you."

We hug each other tight. Then I take a close look at his board. "So this is what you've been working on . . ."

"It's not exactly my best work," he says.

"It looks really interesting."

Ben stands next to me, hands behind his back. "Thanks, it's part of the research from my lab. We're looking at two massive black holes that are merging. You could say they're tangled in a cosmic dance."

"That's really poetic of you," I say.

"I wish I'd come up with it myself."

I learn forward. "What exactly makes it a dance?"

"Notice how they're swirling together," he says, pointing at one of the images. "For a long time, it was believed that black holes orbit each other chaotically. But we recently learned that they're not random at all. Their movements sync up, perfectly aligning in a kind of a waltz that lasts millions of years. It's almost like a love story unfolding in the universe, in a star-crossed kind of way."

"Are you saying they're doomed?"

"In a cosmic sense," he says, folding his arms. "As they draw closer together, they're destined to collide at one point. The gravitational waves are so destructive, it would alter the fabric of space-time as they travel throughout the universe for eternity." He looks at me. "Which is how we are able to detect it and can make these simulations."

I glance at the photo again. "Well, at least they got to share one dance."

"I like that perspective."

We smile at each other. Then I notice something on the table beneath the board. The ceramic tray I made. I secretly left it at his place the last time we were together. I pick it up and say, "Looks like you found the gift I left you."

Ben blushes. "Thought I'd bring it for good luck."

I'm smiling inside. It's nice to know he was thinking of me, too. "I'm glad you like it. Although it is missing a star here . . ." I run my finger over the lines I painted to form a constellation.

"It's perfect the way it is," he says.

People appear to check out his presentation. I step aside to let him do his thing. It's nice seeing him light up from each question. It's obvious how much he cares about his work. I can't help but be a little inspired by this. Maybe I should find something of my own to be passionate about.

The event goes on for another hour. Then he packs up and we leave together. Ben's poster won an award for best visual design. We're going to celebrate with burgers. I tell the waitress it's Ben's birthday to get us a free slice of cake. We share a basket of mozzarella sticks as a woman sings a Kelly Clarkson song in the back of the restaurant.

"I didn't know this place had karaoke," Ben says.

"Do you want to sing something?"

"I might not have it in me after today."

"But you did great," I assure him.

"I still can't believe you came." Ben leans forward, taking me in from across the table. "I was planning to have a frozen dinner alone tonight."

"I borrowed my mom's car. She doesn't need it until the morning." I fold my arms on the table. "Or, technically, in six months. I guess that's true for my assignment that's due, too. Wouldn't that be nice if things stayed that way?"

"Would you actually like that?"

"Of course I would. I mean, wouldn't you?"

"I'm not as sure," he answers. "If anything, I'd want to take a glimpse into the future. A lot can change in six months.

Wouldn't you rather know where your life is headed?"

To be honest, I've never really thought about it. I'm not surprised Ben has though. He's always thinking about his future. He reminds me a lot of Julie in that way, always trying to be ten steps ahead. Meanwhile, there are days I just want everything to pause for a moment.

"I wonder why I can only visit your timeline," I say.

"Yeah. I've thought about that, too."

Maybe there's no point in overthinking all this. After we finish our food, Ben says there's another place he wants to show me. Thankfully, I don't have to make the last bus tonight. It must have rained while we were inside. The lights from the city reflect off the sidewalks. I'm not sure where he's leading me at first. Then the concrete tracks of the monorail appear overhead. It was created for the World's Fair in the early sixties. Ben stops to buy two tickets as we make our way up to the platform. A bridge extends as the monorail's lights appear. It's like stepping into a relic of the past, looking into an old vision of the future.

It's a slow ride through downtown, but the glass windows offer stunning views of the city. Eventually, we arrive at Seattle Center. There's a beautiful garden of glass sculptures that makes us feel like we're on another planet. The Space Needle shines like a spacecraft overhead.

We walk past the International Fountain, watching kids chasing each other around it. Ben leads me up the curved path toward Kerry Park. The lights from Seattle stretch across the sky before us. You can see the Ferris wheel glowing over Pier 57.

I lean against the railing, taking it all in. "The view is *amazing*," I say. "I hope you don't take all your boys here."

"Only you so far," he promises.

"Good."

The sky is especially clear tonight. There are plenty of things to see even without a telescope. According to Ben, certain constellations are more visible at different seasons and depend on where you are in the world. For instance, in the Northern Hemisphere, Orion is most visible in the winter. Meanwhile, Ursa Major can be seen year-round because it rotates around the North Star. You can never miss that big spoon in the sky here in Washington.

"How come we don't see a lot of meteor showers?"

"They depend on the Earth's orbit," Ben explains. "We need to be passing through certain parts of the universe where there's debris left from comets. That's how we always know when to expect them."

I've always thought they were completely random. My brain hurts thinking about the vastness of the universe itself. I think back to Ben's research project. The idea that two giant black holes are dancing billions of light years away from us is unfathomable. "I have a question about something you said earlier. What does it mean to alter the fabric of space-time?"

"That's a tough question," he admits, taking his time to answer. "Have you seen *Interstellar*? It's one of my favorite movies. When the characters travel near a black hole, time works differently. An hour for them equals seven years on Earth. That's because the gravitational forces are so strong, they stretch time itself. Now think about that on a cosmic scale, spreading throughout the universe. Theoretically, if you bend time enough, it should wrap back on itself. A black hole acts like a time machine in that way. Of course, it's just one of a million theories out there."

"Any theories that might explain us?" I ask.

"Not that I know of."

A gust of cold air rolls up the hill, blowing leaves around us. I cross my arms and say, "Looks like we both forgot our jackets this time. Guess it's still spring in my head."

"It's spring in mine, too." Ben smiles at me. "That's another reason I'd want to be six months ahead. I could skip the winter that's coming." He stares to the side, thinking about something. "I'm actually submitting my fellowship application soon. You mentioned looking me up before, right? I was wondering if I got in."

"I don't remember reading about that."

Ben nods. "Maybe it's better not to know. I like *some* surprise in my life."

"Like how I showed up tonight?"

"Exactly."

We smile at each other again. I stare out at the view, taking in the lights from below us. But Ben is still looking at me. "I know I already said this, but I'm really glad you came to see me." He runs a hand through my hair. "I wish we could do this all the time."

"Me too," I say.

"I also wish there was a way *I* could surprise *you*."

It's hard not to think about. "I don't know why it works this way. There are things I wish I could show you. Like this dance next weekend. It would be fun if there was a way you could come. Dress up in a tie, which I see you're accustomed to."

Ben frowns a little. "You should still go, you know?"

"I don't want to go alone."

"Then take someone with you," he suggests. "I don't want

you missing out on things because of me."

"You want me to take someone else?"

"I'm only saying you could if you really wanted to."

"Is that what you want?"

He thinks about it. "No, but I would understand if you did."

I put my arms around him. "I wouldn't want to go with anyone else. Besides, tickets are probably sold out anyway."

Ben pulls me closer to him. His eyes shimmer in the light. "I just don't want either of us to get hurt. What if something happens and we can't see each other again?"

I think about this a lot, too. It's unfair that we had to meet this way. Separated by space and time. Close, but only for a moment.

"I'll fly into a black hole to find you."

Something shoots across the sky, casting a blue light over us. Then Ben leans forward to kiss me. I close my eyes as the rest of the city blinks around us.

CHAPTER EIGHTEEN

"Time is never constant, but always in motion."

Professor Clarke's words have been stuck in my head. Especially these past few days while I'm sitting in class, staring at the clock on the wall. Sometimes, time feels like it's moving faster than I can catch up to it. Like everyone's left on the train while I'm still standing at the platform, waiting. Maybe that's because I don't know which direction I'm going. All these lectures and unfinished assignments haven't helped me figure out what to do with my life. I blink and another day passes without me noticing. No matter how hard I try to slow things down, it feels like time is always running out.

It's been a week since I last saw Ben. It's still hard to believe we're living six months apart. The Pacific Northwest experienced the biggest snowstorm we've had in years, and he doesn't even know it yet. I already received my first grades of the quarter, and he hasn't started classes. I've watched the newest Space Ninjas movie twice, and he's still waiting for it to premiere in theaters. I've been thinking about what Ben said the last time we were together. *"I'd want to take a glimpse into the future . . . Wouldn't you rather know where your life is headed?"*

He's constantly making plans for the future while my head's in the past. Sometimes, it feels like we're looking in different directions. Maybe I should try to think more like him. Have some things in place to look forward to. Like the fellowship he applied to. I wonder if he's heard back by now. I've been doing my best to avoid looking him up again. I don't want to find out these things before him and ruin the surprise. Who knows how that might affect things in the long run?

But I couldn't help myself recently. I googled his name a few days ago. Most of the search results are articles I've seen before. Then I find something dated from two weeks ago. A newsletter from the University of Washington. There's a picture of Ben standing with two other students. Then I read the caption: *Recipients of the ESA Research Award.*

This means he won the fellowship after all. I thought about texting him when I read the rest of the article. *Recipients of this fellowship will have the opportunity to spend up to a year at the Anton Pannekoek Institute for Astronomy in the Netherlands.* I didn't realize he would be *leaving* for so long. What would that mean for us? Living six months apart has been hard enough already. I was hoping we would eventually find a way to fix all this, bridge the timelines somehow so we can finally be together. But how would that be possible when he's on the other side of the world?

I stare at the screen, unsure what to do with the news. I probably shouldn't have looked in the first place. Because now I know what his future looks like. I can't keep it a secret from him, but he did say he wanted some surprises, right? Maybe that means I don't have to tell him right now. I can decide the next time when I see him in person.

Eventually, I force myself to start the day. I'm heading to the shower when something stops me. There are flowers outside my door. A bouquet of beautiful white roses. For a second, I think Ben might have sent them, but that's impossible. How can he send something six months in the future? Maybe they were delivered for Ethan. I glance at the card. It's *my name* written on the envelope. I read the note inside.

Sorry we won't get to dance together tonight.
Feel free to take someone else. —Nolan

He's enclosed two tickets to the Pindar Dance. But why is he giving them to me? I stare at the flowers. I assumed he would have asked someone else to go with him by now. Maybe this is his way of saying he's moved on, too? It's hard to believe we once had plans to go together. At least it's a kind gesture, but I'm not really sure how to feel. He probably remembers how much I was looking forward to it. It's bittersweet in a way I can't put into words.

But what am I supposed to do with these tickets? As much as I want to, it's not like I could take Ben with me. I would give them to Rami, but he's away for the weekend. I wish Julie was here. I know I should probably throw the flowers away, but I hate the thought of them wilting in the garbage. So I bring them inside and place them on my desk.

White roses always remind me of Sam. I once shared that with Nolan, so it's probably not a coincidence that he chose them. He was always thoughtful when it came to my friendship with Sam. It's one of the things I appreciated about him the most.

I should probably give him back the tickets, since I don't have much use for them. Maybe Julie will have an opinion. I take a picture of the flowers and send it to her. Surprisingly, she responds pretty quickly.

> Who are they from?

> Redacted

> Get rid of them

I had a feeling she would say that.

> He also gave me his tickets to the dance tonight

> What a weirdo

> Must be a part of his strategy to win you back

> You better not fall for it

> Maybe but I really don't think it's like that. He gave me BOTH tickets and said I should take someone else

> Hmm. I guess that's nice of him

> But I would still be careful

> Relax. I don't plan on going

> Unless you think I should?

> I suppose it would be a waste...

> You could invite Ben

I glance at the tickets again. If only that was a possibility.

> I don't think he'll make it in time

> That's too bad

> You could always go alone. At least to the dinner portion anyway. Isn't a ticket like two hundred dollars?

I consider this for a moment. Maybe that's not such a bad idea. I could stay for dinner and leave before the actual dance. After all, there's no need to waste both tickets. I should probably run this by Ben first. I know he already said I should go. But it feels wrong to do this without telling him, so I send him a message.

> Got a hold of a ticket to the dance I mentioned!

> I might stop by for a little.
> Food is supposed to be good

> Thoughts?

I wait anxiously for his response. But not for long.

That sounds like fun

Glad you decided to go

> Really wish you could come too

> I'm not planning to go with anyone

> Will probably leave right after dinner

I wish I could be there

It would have been fun to dance together

I close my eyes and try to imagine it. The two of us dressed in suit jackets, surrounded by flowers that decorate the reception hall.

> I know

> Hopefully another time

I'm planning to see my parents for dinner tonight

> Maybe I can drive over afterwards

> For dessert

> Ice cream or something?

I smile at this.

> That sounds great

> Perf

> I'll text you before I leave

It's sad that we can't dance together. At least I get to see him later tonight. Maybe I should have mentioned that Nolan gave me the tickets, but it's not like I'd be *going* with him. I'm sure he won't even be there at all. I'll just go enjoy the dinner and hang out with Ben afterwards. I check the time on my phone. The event doesn't start for a few hours. That gives me plenty of time to get ready.

There's a dress code on the back of the ticket. I'll have to stop by the apartment to grab a change of clothes. As I'm walking through the quad, I notice a line of tents have been set up on the grass. Looks like a club fair is taking place. I've been meaning to sign up for something to do after class. Especially knowing how active Ben is on campus. I glance around at the different tables. There's an astronomy club here that could be fun to join. I could impress Ben with some facts I learn.

I walk up to grab a flyer and key chain. A girl smiles behind the table and says, "Hey, I'm Kat! Our club meets every other Tuesday if you're interested in joining. We're actually having a stargazing event next week. Everyone's welcome to come."

"Oh, really?"

"And it's gonna be a really cool one," she says, smiling. "It's the last chance to see Roy's Comet before it's gone for the next twenty-nine years. We're expecting a big meteor shower that follows it, too. Bring some of your friends if you'd like!"

"Oh, um . . . I don't have really have any friends. But can I have this sticker?"

"Sure."

I've never heard of Roy's Comet before. I wonder if Ben knows about it. I write my name down and check out some of the other tents. Then I head home to grab some things to change into.

The Pindar dinner takes place at Barge Hall. I can hear the music through the open windows. I adjust my tie one more time and make my way inside. Satin-covered tables with floral arrangements fill the room. Maybe I should have gotten here earlier; most of the seats have already been taken. Thankfully, I find a table with two open chairs. I take a seat and scan the rest of the room. I had started to wonder if Nolan might show up to surprise me, but I don't see him or his friends anywhere. I guess these really were the only tickets he had.

Everyone looks like they're dressed for a wedding. A man comes by and fills our water glasses. Then he points to the empty seat, asking if someone is sitting next to me.

"I don't think so," I say.

He nods and clears the table setting. I probably should have just lied. Now everyone here knows I've come dateless. I'm not old enough to be served wine, so they give me some sparkling cider. At least the bread is warm. I smile politely at the couple sitting to my left. They're clearly on a date, so I don't bother starting a conversation. As I'm sipping my drink, someone taps my shoulder.

"Do you mind if I sit here?"

A guy with brown curls stands beside me.

"By all means," I say.

"Cool."

He takes the empty chair to my right. Then he notices the missing table setting.

I lean into him. "They just cleared it a minute ago, but I'm sure they can put it back."

As if on cue, someone comes to reset the table.

"Thanks, sorry." He turns to me and whispers, "I hate being that guy who's late. I thought it started at seven-thirty. I'm Will, by the way."

"I'm Oliver."

"Did you come alone, too?"

I shake my head. "I'm actually dating the head chef. He's in the kitchen now."

"Oh, wow."

I can't hold in the laugh. "I'm kidding. Yeah, it's just me. My ex-boyfriend gave me the tickets, but we broke up a few months ago. Hence the 'ex' before 'boyfriend.'"

"I'm sorry about that," he says.

I wave it off. "Eh, don't be. At least he paid for this dinner. And what about you?"

"I wish I had an ex to pay for dinner. I'm actually third-wheeling right now. But there's no seat over there—" He points to the table to our left. "My bestie is with the guy she's seeing." He leans in and whispers, *"I'm honestly relieved not to sit there. He's kind of an asshole. At least to me."*

"Well, this table has a strict No Asshole policy."

"Thank *god*."

He smiles at me. I notice the blue specks in his eyes in the light. Someone comes around and hands us each a small menu. There are two options for the main course. After some deliberation, Will and I both decide to go with the chicken.

"White meat is better for the environment," he says.

"Cheers to saving the planet."

The first course arrives promptly. It's tomato bisque with a swirl of cream. It's worlds better than the soup that's served in the dining hall. There's a lot of time for guests to chat between courses. Will is a sophomore majoring in political science, though he has no idea what he'll do with that degree after college. "Maybe I'll just go into consulting," he says wearily. "But I don't want to think about that now."

"Yeah. Decide if you want to sell out later."

Thankfully, he laughs at this. There are no fancy restaurants in Ellensburg. That's what makes this dinner so special. The university brings in a famous chef once a year to cook a Michelin star meal, which is what makes the ticket so expensive. The chicken is perfectly seasoned and the side of rosemary potatoes is delicious. Will agrees with me on both points. We're still hungry, so we ask for more bread rolls. Dessert is a slice of chocolate cake, which is the highlight of the night. Dinner ends with champagne, which neither of us can have.

"Should have brought my fake ID," Will sighs.

I shake my head. "Rookie mistake."

"Do you have one, too?"

"With this youthful face?" I say jokingly.

He laughs. "True. No one would believe it."

After dinner is over, we rise from our seats. "Are you also heading to the dance?" Will asks me. "Or the 'reception,' or whatever they're calling it."

"Yeah, I'll come for a bit."

Will smiles. "Cool. I'll see you there." Then he heads off to meet his friends.

Maybe we should have exchanged numbers or something. I'm sure I'll see him in a few minutes anyway. I was planning to head back to the dorm after dinner, but Ben texted me a few minutes ago, letting me know he's running late. So I might as well stop by the reception, which is taking place in the ballroom of the Student Union,to kill some time. I've heard there's usually good music. And I'm curious to see what the vibe is like.

★ ★ ★

Purple lights shine from a DJ booth in the corner. Phoebe Bridgers is playing through the giant speakers on the walls. I've never been inside the ballroom before. There's already a good amount of people, but I don't see Will anywhere. There are a few high-top tables that are covered with plastic petals. I stand beside one and take in the crowd from a distance.

I didn't realize how many students would be here. Half the room is dancing while the other half is standing around, chatting in small circles. Someone tosses a beach ball into the center of the room. Another song comes on, but I don't leave my spot at the table. I would be having more fun if Ben was here. I should really try to enjoy myself though. There's no reason to feel guilty about having a good time, right? Since Ben still hasn't arrived, I'd just be sitting in my dorm alone anyway. I'll just stay for another ten minutes and head out.

You can only be a wallflower for so long. I thought I would have run into Will by now. Maybe he's in the bathroom or something. I know we haven't known each other long, but I was hoping to at least say goodbye and that it was nice to meet him. So I make my way through the crowd. The shifting lights make it difficult to recognize faces. There's a chance I walked right past him. As I continue through the crowd, the music changes to a familiar song . . .

"Fade into You," by Mazzy Star. One of Sam's favorites.

A memory swims to the surface. This is the song that was playing when I was looking for Sam at the school dance. My stomach sank when I found him outside, dancing with someone who wasn't me. Of course, that someone was Julie. We didn't really know each other yet. I remember clutching the white rose he'd pinned to my jacket before heading back inside.

Maybe that's enough music for tonight. Ben should probably be here soon anyway.

As I'm finally heading out, a hand grabs my shoulder. I turn around to see who it is.

"Oh—Will!"

He smiles. "Hey, are you leaving already?"

"No, I was just. . . . Were you here the whole time?"

"Yeah, my friends are up there." He points toward the DJ

booth. "Where's your group?"

"Uh, it's just me right now."

"Oh, nice. What do you think so far?"

"Music's not bad. Anyone who plays Phoebe Bridgers deserves a raise."

"Oh my god, that was my request."

"Really? Glad to know *someone* has taste."

He stands there for a moment. I can tell he wants to ask me something. Eventually he leans in and asks, "Do you want to dance?"

I hesitate. His blue-green eyes make it hard to say no. I mean, maybe one dance wouldn't hurt, right? But I don't think I can do that to Ben. I feel bad about turning down Will, especially when he's been so nice. "I'm sorry, but I can't. I'm seeing someone right now."

"Oh . . . I didn't know."

"Sorry. I should have mentioned—"

"No, it's cool."

There's an awkward silence. I check the time on my phone. There's a new message from Ben. "I should probably head out," I say. "But it was nice meeting you."

Will smiles. "For sure. Guess I'll see you around."

I feel guilty about leaving abruptly, but I don't know what else to say. I wasn't planning to stay this long anyway. I head out the door before someone else notices me.

It's starting to rain outside. Ben says he'll be here in a few minutes. I told him I would wait for him near the bridge we met on. I wish I had brought an umbrella with me, but I just ignore the rain as I take a seat on the bench. Thankfully, it's only a sprinkle. And it feels nice against my skin. I close my eyes for a moment and listen to the soft hum of the lights above the empty street.

I'm not sure how much time passes as I'm waiting. And then everything goes quiet for a moment. The rain seems to soften and the temperature drops. I open my eyes again. It's snowing, the flakes lightly brushing my face.

Someone is sitting beside me.

I turn my head. "Ben. When did you. . . ."

He smiles at me. "Only a moment ago." Then he leans forward, brushing something off my face. "You're all wet."

I let out a breath. "I looked better an hour ago."

"I like you this way." The touch of his hand warms me up. He's wearing a dark green coat, and his hair is lightly dusted with snow. "Sorry for bringing the cold with me."

"It's okay. I like the snow."

"I've never seen you this dressed up."

I laugh a little. "Glad someone appreciates the tie. I had to look up a video tutorial."

"It really suits you," he says. "Sorry I couldn't come to your dance."

"Don't apologize. Technically, it hasn't even happened yet."

"That might be true. But I wish I could have."

I don't say anything.

"Hopefully, you still had a good time," he says.

"It was alright. Was thinking of you the whole time."

"I should make it up to you, then."

"I mean, I was sitting in the snow waiting for you," I agree.

Ben smiles as he rises from the bench. Then he slowly removes his jacket.

"What are you doing?" I ask.

"Didn't want you to feel overdressed." Beneath his jacket

is a nice button-up collared shirt.

I narrow my eyes. "What are you about to do . . ."

"I felt bad about missing your formal," he says, setting down his jacket. "Admittedly, I wasn't planning to do this outside, but we can still share a dance."

"*Ben.*"

"*Oliver.*"

That charming smirk curves along his face. Then he takes out his phone. I watch as he picks a song and then sets the phone down on the bench. Of course, it's Joni Mitchell. Ben holds out a hand, helping me off the bench. Admittedly, I'm a little shy about doing this in public. What if someone from class sees this? Ben puts a hand around me, pulling me into him. The snow falls gently around us as we move slowly to the music. It only takes a minute for the nerves to fade away.

Ben moves his lips to my ear. "*I know this isn't quite the same . . .*"

"No, *it's better*," I say.

For a moment, I don't care if anyone sees us. We're the only two people in the world. As the songs change, I tell myself to remember each one. I'll add them to the soundtrack we're slowly building. I know we're still figuring out how we can make this work, but I don't want to think about that. None of that matters right now. We'll find a way to have more dances together.

CHAPTER NINETEEN

The snow continues to fall in the Ellensburg Ben and I share. Thankfully, it's not cold enough for it to stick to the ground. We make the most of the few hours we have together. I'd forgotten how beautiful everything is with the lights that decorate campus this time of year. We grab some hot drinks from the Student Union and find a place to stay warm. I show Ben one of the common rooms that has a fireplace going during the winter. We play a few board games and listen to music. I think he lets me win the last two rounds of Bananagrams.

I wish we could hang out all night together. But I know that, eventually, he has to return to Seattle. I hate that he lives so far away. If only I had a place for him to stay.

"When do you have to leave again?" I ask.

Ben glances at the time. "Maybe soon. I shouldn't be driving back *too* late."

I frown. "Sorry I don't have my own place."

"Where are you staying tonight?"

"Probably on my mom's sofa. Don't wanna go back to my old dorm." I recall breaking into the girl's room last time. Thank god nothing bad came out of that.

"Why don't you come back with me instead?"

"Really?"

"Unless you're too tired . . ."

"You know I'm not," I say.

Ben smiles. "Good. Because I'm not either."

I was hoping he might ask me to come back with him. We only get to see each other once a week. Why should we waste the rest of the night? The snow has stopped when we come outside. Ben turns on the radio as we drive down the highway. The time honestly flies by when we're together, singing along to the music. We park the car across the street and walk up to his apartment. I change into one of his shirts while he grabs me some water from the kitchen. The Polaroid of me is still there on the wall.

There's no television in Ben's room. He takes out his laptop and picks a movie for us to watch. Of course, we're not really paying close attention to it. I'm too busy appreciating how soft his hands are. He looks so beautiful in the glow of the streetlight outside his window. I take in the contours of his face, the waves in his hair, the scent of cologne that lingers on his tan skin. I want to memorize every feature, in case everything vanishes in the morning. Ben kisses my forehead. Then, slowly, he moves his lips to mine. After, he reaches over me and closes the blinds.

He lays his head on me and we fall asleep together.

⋆ ⋆ ⋆

When I wake up in the morning, something is different. Maybe it's the way the light warms the side of my face. Or the way the blanket feels against my skin. It doesn't take long to realize—I'm not in my own bed. That's when I sense something else. The sound of another person breathing. I open my eyes and find Ben sleeping next to me. His fingers are gently touching my side. I take this in, unsure why I'm here.

Shouldn't I be back in Ellensburg?

I must have woken him up, because he blinks his eyes open and stares at me. His voice is scratchy when he says, "Oliver. . . . What time is it?"

"I'm not sure . . ."

"This isn't a dream, is it?"

"I was wondering the same thing."

Ben touches my face as if to check if I'm real. "You're usually already gone when I wake up."

I'm not sure what's different this time. I return the touch, running my fingers along his arm. Then we smile at each other. I've never seen him in the morning glow before.

We stay like that, facing each other, until one of our alarms goes off. Then we both rise up from the bed.

Ben checks his phone first. "It's 10:15 already."

"That's pretty early for me. What day is it?"

"The first of December." He holds out his screen for me to see.

I stare at the date. "I can't believe I didn't disappear this time."

"You know what that means, don't you?"

"No, what?"

He kisses my nose. "I can finally cook you breakfast."

I smile as he opens the blinds, letting in more sunlight. I can't believe this is actually happening. Ben pulls me up from the bed and hands me a pair of shorts from his dresser.

Then I follow him into the kitchen, where he opens the fridge and says, "Luckily, I went grocery shopping yesterday."

"It's like you knew this would happen . . ."

"Honestly, but I hoped it would."

I offer to be his sous chef, but Ben insists on doing everything. I think he wants to surprise me with his skills in the kitchen. So I pull out a chair at the little dining table. Ben puts on his morning playlist and hums along to it. He pours me some coffee and says, "And how do you like your eggs? Sunny side up, scrambled, or fancy?"

"Oh, *definitely* fancy."

"Great choice." He winks at me.

It's fun watching him cook in his white apron. You can tell how much he loves it from the neatly labeled ingredients in the cupboard. Eventually, he lets me help out, and I cut scallions while he rinses the rice and turns on the stove. I imagine us living together someday. Cooking breakfast like this every morning. Adding more Polaroids to the wall. Watching the sun rise and set from the fire escape.

Ben holds the pan at an angle as he stirs the eggs, using a flicking motion. Then he lays the eggs over a small bed of rice and slices them down the center, revealing a silky interior. He sets the plate in front of me. "This is called *omurice*," he says.

"It's like I woke up to a five-star restaurant."

"Welcome to Chez Ben," he says with a graceful bow.

He lets me take the first bite. It tastes even better with the sliced avocado he also prepared. Ben tells me he likes to save recipes he finds online. He grew up cooking with his mom at home. It's his favorite thing to do when he wants to take his mind off schoolwork.

"If the astronomy thing doesn't work out, you would be a great chef," I tell him and take another sip of coffee. "You know what they say . . . whether a poet looks through a pantry or telescope, he always sees the same thing."

"Is that a real quote?"

"I might have revised it a little."

He smiles. "And what's it supposed to mean, exactly?"

"It means you see the possibility in things," I say confidently. "Regardless of what you do. Everything's a universe, if you *really* think about it."

"I like that," he says, nodding. "Maybe you should major in philosophy."

"Don't know if I'm smart enough for that."

"I think you're smarter than you think you are."

I don't say anything back because I'm not used to hearing people say this about me.

We finish breakfast, but we stay at the table, enjoying each other's company. Of course, I don't want to intrude on his entire day. Ben has several assignments that are due this week. His notes are spread out across the coffee table. But it feels like the universe gave us extra time. Maybe we shouldn't let it go to waste.

Ben notices me looking at his unfinished work. He puts it away and says, "I can finish this later. Let's find something fun to do!"

"Procrastinating on schoolwork? Sounds like I'm rubbing off on you."

"I'm allowed to take breaks," he says, shrugging it off. "Since you're already here, I can show you more of Seattle. Maybe convince you to move here someday."

"You really want me to stay, don't you?"

Ben smiles and kisses me on the lips. Eventually, I help him wash the dishes and put everything away. I only have my suit jacket with me. So he lets me borrow a coat. Then we head outside and take a stroll through the neighborhood. Ben shows me his favorite bookstore with a secret door in the back that leads to a sandwich shop. We grab some hot chocolate and walk around the park together. A woman lets us pet her goldendoodle. Then we take the bus to Pier 57 to watch the boats pass. He wins a keychain of a goldfish for me at the arcade. I've been on the Ferris wheel before, but it feels different with him. We hold hands as we're lifted into the sky. I've lost track of how many times he stopped to steal a glance at me.

I wish we could spend every day together. I don't want to keep waking up without him. This must be what it feels like to fall in love without saying the word. The way he stares at me says he's thinking the same. I don't know why we were connected this way, but I like to believe there's a reason for it. Maybe we're part of some cosmic story, stretching throughout the universe. I just hope it has a good ending.

As much as I want time to stay frozen, eventually I need to head back home. Ben walks me to the bus station and waits with me. He pulls me in for a long hug and kisses me before I have to go.

"I wish you didn't live . . . so far," he whispers.

"Seriously."

He kisses me again. "I'm not sure how, but I hope we can do this again someday."

"I hope so, too." I've never felt closer to him.

Then I step onto the bus headed back to Ellensburg. For the first time, I'm certain that one day, we'll get to truly be together.

CHAPTER TWENTY

I wake up with an ache on my neck and shoulder. It often happens when I sleep on the sofa at the apartment. I texted Mom last night, letting her know I was staying over. It was still fall when I returned from Seattle. The timeline usually changes when I wake up in the morning. I don't exactly understand the way it works. Especially after yesterday. But I wasn't planning to go back to my old dorm with Connor. I open my eyes slowly and the room comes into focus.

For some reason, I'm still on Mom's sofa. I thought I would have woken up in my own bed by now. I check the calendar on my phone—December 2. What am I still doing in Ben's timeline? Eventually, I send him a text message.

> So . . . update

> I haven't gone back yet

> Not really sure what's different this time

Thankfully, he's already awake.

> What do you mean?

> I usually wake up in my own timeline

> But it's still the fall for me

> Huh that's really weird

> Maybe it's just taking longer than usual

> Yeah, I'm sure you're right

I just have to give it some more time. That's not necessarily a bad thing. I can pretend none of my assignments are due. I get up and take a look around the apartment. Mom must have left for work already. What am I supposed to do with the day though? I guess I could watch some television to kill the time.

Then I remember something. Julie should still be in town. That means I can spend some time with her. I try to pull up her location, but my phone is being weird today. The screen keeps blacking out when I open an app. It probably just needs another restart. At least I can still text her.

> Hi! What are you up to?

Julie doesn't respond right away. So I text her again.

> Julieeeeeeee
>
> Answer meeeeeee

Hey, having breakfast

> WHERE?

Dining hall

She doesn't have to tell me twice. I throw on some clothes and head there immediately. I breathe in the morning chill as I make my way to campus. It feels like ages since we've sat down for a meal together. I've been mostly eating by myself these past few weeks. I head through the doors and spot her right away. She's sitting near the soda fountain, reading a book. I run up and squeeze her from behind.

"*Julie . . . Ugh, I missed you.*"

She groans. "Not this again."

"It's like a gift from the universe." I hold on to her for a few more seconds. Then I pull out the seat next to her, smiling uncontrollably.

"Why are you acting like we don't hang out every day," she says.

"Can't I just be happy to see you?"

"If you need to copy off of my assignment, just say so."

I should probably tone it down a little, but I can't help myself. "I just want to hang out with my best friend. Is that a *crime*?"

Julie rolls her eyes. "If you can't tell, I'm studying right now."

I take her book and set it down. "You can take a break, okay? Let's do something fun instead. You know, for old times' sake."

"Like what?"

"I don't know, anything you want." What are some activities we could do together? It's probably too late for apple picking. "We could take a walk through the bird sanctuary. Or visit the Historical Museum."

"You hate that museum," she says.

"But I know *you* love it."

She narrows her eyes. "Do you need to borrow my car or something?"

"*No*, I don't need anything! I just want to spend time together."

"Alright, fine. I'll go."

"Good. Because I wasn't taking no for an answer."

I could honestly just sit here and watch her read, but when is the next time we'll get to have an Oliver-and-Julie day? We should make the most of this. I help Julie finish her food by eating the rest of it. We can grab coffee at Sun and Moon first. Then stop by Mr. Lee's bookstore for a visit. As we're heading into town, I remember something else. My favorite bakery is still open.

"Wait," I gasp. "We need to stop for a chocolate croissant. I haven't had one in *ages*."

"Oliver. You had one yesterday. I was with you."

I ignore this and pull her down the street. The sugary-sweet scent fills the air as we come inside. I didn't buy anything the last time I was here with Ben. I get a box of my favorite things, which includes a dozen macarons. Julie and I take a bite of each flavor and split the chocolate croissant.

I've missed having her around. It reminds me how hard the quarter has been without her. She eventually embraces my clinginess, attributing it to the holiday season. We walk through the Christmas market that's decorated with lights. We spend the afternoon there, drinking hot apple cider and looking at all of the handmade jewelry. Then we grab a late lunch at Sweet Juice.

I offer to stop by the museum afterward, but Julie has to head home to help her mom prep for dinner. She says we can meet up again later tonight. I walk her home and then head back to campus. I'm so happy to get another day in this timeline. There's no schoolwork to stress about. And I get to see my best friend again. Wouldn't it be nice if I got to stay longer?

I walk through the quad, enjoying the brisk weather. Though I wish I had a warmer jacket. Maybe I could stop by my old dorm for a second and grab something from my closet. Let's hope my old roommate won't be there. There's a good chance he's at the Student Union around at this time of day.

I check my phone. There's a text message from Mom.

> See you in an hour

> Can't wait for the class

What is she talking about? I'm about to text back when it hits me. Oh my god, it's December 2. Mom's birthday is today! I can't believe I forgot about it. That means our pottery class is tonight. Mom said it was the best present she'd received in her four decades of life. She uses the dish we made together every day. It would be nice to get to experience that with her again.

And then I remember something else—it's also the night of Nolan's party. The same night someone saw him leave with his hand wrapped around Connor. All this happened while I was celebrating Mom's birthday. I've tried hard to separate those two memories. As the emotions flood back, something else occurs to me.

Doesn't this mean it hasn't happened yet?

I check my last messages. Nolan's party should already have started. They always start drinking early on Sundays. I stare at the ground, knots in my stomach. This is something I've been trying so hard to forget. Now here it is about to happen all over again.

I've replayed this night in my head a thousand times. What would have happened if I had gone to the party instead? Maybe I could have prevented it somehow . . . Is that even a possibility? It's not that I want Nolan back, but I could save myself from so much pain . . .

There's another text from Mom.

> Do you want me to pick you up?

I consider the options. I can't abandon Mom on her birthday. Because of her work schedule, I signed us up for the evening class, but it doesn't start for another hour. Maybe I could stay at the party until then? Hopefully she won't be too upset if I'm a little late. But how often do you get the chance to fix the past?

I send Mom a quick text.

> I'll meet you at the ceramics place!
>
> Have something I need to do first

I hesitate on the sidewalk, unsure of this. Then I turn around and head to the party.

Nolan and his friends always host their parties in the basement of someone's dorm building. They can get out of hand sometimes. But Sundays are usually more chill, so I'm not surprised to see it half filled at the moment. It's strange walking in here after all these months. A few of his friends are setting up a game of beer pong. They're playing some Kendrick song I don't recognize. Then someone comes up behind me, covering my eyes with their hands. But I recognize the scent of Acqua di Giò.

I turn around to face him. Nolan is wearing his usual white muscle shirt that always looks great on him. His blond waves are particularly lustrous tonight.

"Hey there, cutie," he says. "Thought you couldn't come tonight."

I'm not sure how to respond. "Just thought I'd stop by for a minute."

He smiles and kisses me on the cheek. "So what you're saying is, you can't stop thinking about me. Want something to drink? We have your favorite strawberry seltzer."

I hate how sweet he treated me. I shake the thought out of my head and say, "I'm not thirsty."

"Come on. Just one drink."

Nolan puts a hand on my shoulder, walking me over to the bar. His friends appear to greet us. It's weird being surrounded by them again. I'm not really listening to what they say. I keep scanning the room to see if Connor is here yet.

"Who are you looking for?" Nolan asks.

"*Nobody*," I say, somewhat tensely. "Just seeing who else is here."

"Want some pretzels? Zach stole some from the dining hall."

"Not really."

"You probably haven't eaten yet. I'll grab some for you anyway."

I let out a breath and he walks off. Then I glance around the room again. More people come down the stairs, but I don't see Connor anywhere. The minutes are ticking away. Maybe that traitor of a roommate plans to arrive when he knows I'll be at the ceramics class. I'll have to leave soon for that. As I'm keeping an eye out, an idea comes to me. I send Julie a message, asking here to come here.

> What for?

> Just do it for me

Nolan returns with some pretzels before his attention is pulled to the door as more people arrive. I set the plastic plate on the speaker and wait for Julie, but I really can't stay much longer. I check the time again—the class started a few minutes ago. I need to get going already.

Someone taps on my shoulder.

"*Julie.* There you are!"

"Why isn't your location working—"

"I don't know. My phone's being weird. But that's not important right now."

"Aren't you supposed to be with your mom?"

"*Yes*," I say, pulling her to the side. "Which is why I asked you to come here. I really need you to do me a favor."

"What is it?"

"I need you to keep an eye on Nolan."

She gives me a look. "*Why?*"

"It's hard to explain, but I have reasons not to trust him tonight."

"Is there something you're not telling me?"

I let out a breath. "*Please just do it.* I really have to go."

"Alright. I'll stay but—"

"Thank you."

I give her a hug before heading out the door. I can always count on Julie, even when I'm keeping things from her. I really should have left sooner. Especially since I don't have a car. I'm sprinting through campus, sending Mom more texts. There's no time to wait for the next bus to come—I have to run the entire way there.

It takes much longer to get to the pottery place than I expected. The class is just ending when I walk in. People are putting on jackets and packing up their things, but I don't see my mom. Did she leave already? I look out the window. Her car isn't parked outside. I can't believe I actually missed it. I ruined her special birthday. I linger outside, in case she still around. Eventually, someone turns the lights off and locks the door. So I head to the bus stop.

It's late when I get back to her apartment. I'm hoping Mom is sitting at the table, expecting an apology. But she's not waiting for me, and the door to her room is closed. I didn't even get a chance to wish her a happy birthday. She'd been looking forward to this for weeks. She must be so disappointed in me. I consider knocking on her door, but I don't want to wake her. Especially if she's upset with me right now. The memory we once made is gone now. I should have never gone to that dumb party.

CHAPTER TWENTY-ONE

I'm hoping yesterday was a dream. I open my eyes to the sunlight. I'm not back in my dorm room. I'm still on Mom's sofa, where I slept last night. How much longer will I be here?

I push myself up and look at the time. Mom must have left for work early again, because the car keys are gone from the hook. My mind goes back to last night. I can't believe what I did yesterday. I didn't even stay long enough to see Connor at the party. Why was that so important to me? I don't even know if it changed anything.

There are no new messages from Julie. Maybe that means Nolan and Connor didn't leave together this time. Strangely, I don't feel much better about it, even if I did manage to stop it from happening. I stare at the clouds through the window. It's another day in Ben's timeline. I wish we could at least spend it together. But I'm sure he's busy with class today.

And it's not like he lives across the street from me. I need to find Julie and ask her about the party. I send her a quick text. She doesn't respond, but I have a feeling I know where she is anyway.

I grab a jacket and take a brisk stroll through campus. I tried looking up Julie's location earlier. The screen still glitches when I open the app. But I don't really need it to know where she is. I head to the library. Julie usually studies there in the morning before class. I find her sitting at her favorite table by the window. There are a few other people studying here. I try to keep quiet and take the seat next to her.

Julie looks up and says, "Morning."

"Had a feeling you'd be here," I say proudly.

"It *is* Monday. Might need another coffee soon." She tucks her hair behind her ear. "How was your mom's birthday last night?"

I lean back in my chair, sighing. "I missed it."

"What do you mean, *you missed it*?"

"I didn't make it in time," I whisper. "I know, it's stupid. I was stupid."

Julie closes her book. "*Oliver*, I can't believe you. What did your mom say about it?"

"I haven't talked to her yet. She left before I woke up."

"Was it because you stopped by that party? I don't know why you went in the first place." She shakes her head in disappointment.

"I was only there for an hour. Did anything happen after I left?"

"Not really," she says, thinking about it. "Except Nolan's friend Tony was flirting with me the whole time."

"What about Connor? Did he show up?"

"At one point. But he didn't stay long."

"Did Nolan leave with him?"

"No, he was with me the whole time," she says.

"So you don't think anything *happened*?"

"Not that I could tell." She leans forward, keeping her voice low. "*Is something going on between them?*"

I let out a breath. "*Maybe*."

"What makes you think that?"

"Woman's intuition," I say vaguely.

"Stop being so cryptic and tell me."

"I can't really say. I just had a . . . feeling, okay?"

Julie presses her lips together. "Well, if it's only a *feeling*, why don't you just talk to Nolan about it?"

I give her a look. "Why on earth would I talk to that jerk?"

"I mean, you are dating him," she reminds me.

"Oh. Right."

I almost forgot about that part. This shouldn't bother me so much. Especially after all the healing I've done. Who cares what happened after the party? It won't change what I have with Ben. I push last night out of my mind and say, "Forget Nolan. I don't want to talk about him anymore."

"You're so moody lately," Julie says.

"I just need something to eat."

"Aren't you supposed to be in class?"

I blink at her. "*Class?*"

"It's Monday. Don't you have Math Modeling?"

Then it hits me—this is fall quarter. What was my schedule again? It takes a second to come back to me. "Oh my god, you're right."

Does this mean I'm supposed go? I rise from my chair and make my way out anyway. I thought I would never step foot in the math building again. I'm not sure if it affects my own timeline if I skip it. But I don't want to take any risks and fail the class. I've had plenty of nightmares about this very scenario. I'm only fifteen minutes late when I come through the door. Thankfully, it's a pretty big lecture hall. I find an empty seat as Professor Paul seems not to notice and continues to write on the board.

I can't believe I have to listen to this all over again. Professor Paul is going over differential equations. I barely understood it the first time around. I had to go to office hours for help every week. I don't even have anything to take notes with. So I just sit there and try not to look confused.

The hour goes by painfully slow. I'm counting down the minutes until it's over. At the end of class, Professor Paul reminds us about the assignment that's due. There's no way I have to do that, right? I don't even remember where my textbook is. Thankfully, the person next to me lets me borrow a pen. I write the page number on my hand and head out.

I try to remember the rest of my schedule. I only took Math Modeling to fulfill the core requirement. Hopefully I don't have to come back tomorrow. Should I be worrying about my classes though? Maybe I'll grab my books, just in case. That would mean stopping by my old dorm room.

As I'm coming out of the building, someone is waiting for me.

"*Hey.*"

I stop abruptly. I forgot Nolan always waits for me after class. He smiles and leans in for a kiss. But I manage to dodge it this time. He blinks at me and says, "Is everything good?"

"Yeah, fine."

"I tried calling this morning," he says.

"Sorry. It's my phone."

"Are we still getting lunch later?"

I shake my head. "No, I have to study."

"You still need some food, right?"

"I'm, uh, also sick." I pretend to cough. "Gotta go now."

I turn abruptly and hurry off. It doesn't matter if we're still together in this timeline. I still don't want anything to do with him. I cross the bridge, heading toward my old dorm. I'm hoping I can just grab my things and go.

Luckily, Connor isn't there when I come in. The books are sitting on my desk beside the succulent I never watered. I only take the textbooks I think I need. And I might as well grab some clothes while I'm here. Especially since I have no plans to come back later. I place everything into a bag and head for the door.

But I pause and stare at Connor's side of the room. I'm still not sure if something happened between him and Nolan last night. There could be some clues around here. I imagine finding Nolan's boxers or wallet beneath the sheets. I know I shouldn't care anymore, but something inside me says to check. So I lift them up and take a quick look. I don't find anything suspicious. Unless it fell down the side of the bed.

As I'm climbing over the mattress, the door opens behind me.

Connor comes into the room. He takes his headphones off and watches me scramble off the bed. This obviously looks suspicious.

"Lose something there?"

"Uh, no?"

"What are you doing on my bed?"

I could easily make something up. But I might as well

confront him about it. After all, I've already done it once before. I straighten myself and say, "Did you hook up with Nolan?"

His expression freezes. "When did he tell you . . ."

My stomach turns. I'm feeling sick again. "So that was your plan all along? To wait until I was gone last night?"

He blinks, confused. "We didn't hook up last night."

"Then when did it happen?"

"Like a month ago."

"A *month ago?* How long has this been going on?"

"It was only the one time," he says.

I can't believe what I'm hearing. How could it have already happened? I'm about to go on a tirade, calling him the worst roommate in the world, but this confrontation is no longer worth my time. So I grab my bag and leave without another word. As I'm out the door, I remember something. The last time I left, I took back the MALIN+GOETZ candle I bought him during a sale. This is one thing I want to repeat. I head back inside and grab it from his dresser.

"I'm taking my gift back."

Then I storm out again. I'm not really sure where to go anymore. I turn down the road and make my way off campus.

There's a spot behind the park I used to go to as a kid. It's a small hiding place, shrouded by trees and bushes. When I was younger, I used to come here when my parents were arguing. It became my secret escape from the world. Like Sophie's garden in *Howl's Moving Castle*. Or the creek by the woods in *Bridge to Terabithia*. The last time I came here was the day after Sam's funeral. He was one of the few people who knew about this place. Maybe I watched too many movies growing up. It's magical thinking, but a part of me wondered whether he might show up if I waited long enough.

There's a rustle in the bushes followed by a voice calling out my name.

"Oliver?"

Crawling on her hands and knees, Julie emerges from the fortress of branches. I sent her a long text an hour ago while she was in class. I had to tell someone about what happened earlier. I'm still processing it as she sits down next to me.

"What are you doing out here?"

"Being a prisoner of my own thoughts."

Julie sighs. "Usually, I'd call you dramatic, but I think you have a right to be this time." I've already told her about Nolan, at least the part that Connor revealed to me. "I'm sorry about what happened."

I say nothing.

"How did you find out about it?"

"It doesn't really matter right now."

She frowns. "I'm sorry I didn't do a better job yesterday."

"Don't be. It wouldn't have changed anything."

I silently pick at the dry grass. Julie watches me for a while. Then she says, "I'm surprised you're not taking this harder."

That's because I technically found out about this six months ago. Maybe I thought it would hurt less if I could stop it. I should have just showed up for Mom's birthday or spent another night with Ben instead of wasting time trying to change the past. All I can think to say is, "It's not the worst loss I've experienced."

My words hang in the air.

Julie touches my shoulder. "Forget Nolan. I never liked him anyway."

"I know you didn't."

We sit there for a while, listening to the branches brushing against each other. Julie helped me go through this the first time around. I wonder what future her from the spring would say to me. Probably something I don't want to hear right now.

Eventually, Julie helps me up to my feet. Then she walks me back to campus.

At least we get to spend more time together. It reminds me how much I've missed her lately. We grab some food from the dining hall and head to the library. I don't bother to study for anything. But watching her write makes it feel like old times again. Who knows how much longer I'll be here, so I try to enjoy the hours we have together.

But I'm still here when I wake up the next morning.

And I'm here the day after that.

I'm starting to think that I'm not going back.

CHAPTER TWENTY-TWO

It's a whirlwind of a school week. I'm trying to pin down my schedule as I sit through my old classes. I never thought I'd have to memorize the geologic time scale again. I don't remember where any of my notes are. Is it really possible I'm stuck here? And I have to take all my finals again? I was freaking out about that, but some things have started to come back to me. Like memories, filling the gaps in my head. Maybe it's not the end of the world if I stay. Who wouldn't want to redo the last six months of their life? Especially if it means being closer to someone you love.

Ben is coming to see me later. It's been difficult making plans over text since my phone is still acting up. I've had to restart it several times this morning. I wish I could just call to hear the sound of his voice. But it doesn't matter, because at least this means I'll get to spend more time with him. After all, he's the main reason I'm back here. Right?

We're planning to meet up after class. I wanted to introduce him to Mom at our Thursday dinner, but she isn't really speaking to me. She canceled dinner tonight and took an extra shift at the restaurant. I know she's still upset about me missing her birthday. I wish she would give me a chance to make it up to her.

At least Julie is still around. I've missed her so much. I know she and Ben already met briefly, but I can't wait for her to start actually getting to know him. We're all going to grab some food in town when he arrives. I invited her this morning, when I met her at the library again. She was sitting at her usual spot, staring silently out the window. There was something so sad and lonely about it. I wonder what she was thinking about.

It was always her plan to leave Ellensburg. She never really liked it here, which I don't blame her for. Especially after Sam died. I know she'll be in Copenhagen in the spring, but it feels like I've trapped her into some temporary limbo with me. I remember how happy she sounded over the phone. I almost miss hearing all the stories she shared about her travels. I'm trying not to think about it too much. It's not like there's anything I can do about it now.

I'm meeting Ben outside of Sun and Moon. I know it hasn't actually been that long since we saw each other, but these last few days have felt like months. My body floods with happiness when I turn the corner and see Ben standing on the sidewalk, holding flowers. A smile blooms across his face, and

YOU'VE FOUND OLIVER

I wrap my arms around him, pressing myself against him. All my stress falls away when we're together. I breathe in the familiar scent on his shirt. Then I glance at the flowers and say, "Are those for me?"

"Oh, no. They're actually for Julie."

"You brought them for *Julie*?"

"I want to make sure to leave a good impression," he says. "Since I know her opinion is important to you."

"Oh, that's sweet of you. But I like flowers, too, you know?" I crack a smile. "Besides, I'm sure she'll love you no matter what. You guys actually have a lot in common."

"Hopefully. Are we waiting for her here?"

"She had to stop at home first." I check my phone again. "She says she'll meet us at the diner. You'll like it. They serve breakfast all day."

"Hopefully not as good as mine," he says, smiling. "I'm actually starving though."

Mo's is your typical small-town diner. It's changed names and owners several times over the years, but the décor pretty much stays the same. Round barstools, checkered linoleum floors, a jukebox playing in the corner. We sit close together on the same side of the booth, and Ben tells me about his busy week at school. The research project he's working on in the lab might get published next year.

"The one about black holes?" I ask.

Ben nods. "It's being reviewed right now, so we'll see where it goes."

Finally, Julie comes through the door. She takes a seat on the other side of the booth and sighs. "Sorry I'm late. I had to help my mom check the house for microphones. She thinks the government is listening to us again." She smiles politely at Ben. "Hi. I believe we've already met."

Ben smiles back. "Only briefly. Apologies for interrupting your date last time," he says.

I shrug. "Eh, never liked the guy anyway. Scottie, right?"

"His name was *Craig*."

"Whatever."

"Oliver mentioned you're from Seattle," Ben says.

Julie nods. "Yeah, I grew up there."

"I think I can tell."

"Is that so? I'm guessing you're from there, too, then."

"No, but I go to the University of Washington."

"Oh, really?" she says, leaning into the table. "Both my parents graduated from there. That's actually where they met. What are you studying?"

"Astronomy."

"Interesting." Julie glances between us. "Remind me how you guys met?"

I should probably answer this one, but I'm curious to see what he comes up with, so I lean back and say teasingly, "Yeah, Ben. Why don't you tell her the story."

Ben blinks at me. "You want *me* to answer?" He takes a second to think. "Wer . . . met at a research conference."

Julie raises a brow. "Oliver . . . at a *research conference*? Did he wander in there by accident or something?"

I shoot her a look. "What's that supposed to mean?"

"Oliver actually knows a lot about space," Ben says, touching my shoulder. "At least in the abstract sense. He came up to my presentation on black holes and asked a lot of thoughtful questions."

Julie points to me. "*This* Oliver?"

I throw up my hands. "What's so hard to believe?"

"I just didn't know you were interested in astronomy," she says, shrugging.

"Then maybe you don't know me as well as you *think* you do."

The waitress comes to take our order. As usual, Julie orders a Greek salad with a side of fries. Ben and I are going to share the country fried steak and a blueberry waffle. The moment the waitress walks off, Julie notices the flowers.

"Whose are those?" she asks, pointing.

"Actually, they're for you." Ben hands them to her.

"Oh . . . really?"

"Oliver mentioned you like roses, too."

"I do. But what are they for?"

I fold my arms. "Does there need to be a reason?"

"You're right. That's really kind of you. Thank you."

She holds the flowers like she's not sure what to do with them.

There's an awkward silence. Thankfully, Ben breaks it by saying, "So, Oliver tells me you're studying abroad in the spring."

"Actually, I might not be going."

I look at her. "What are you talking about?"

"I'm sure you'll be happy to hear this," she says, setting the flowers down beside her. "But I'll probably being staying here after all. My dad's accepting a position in Baltimore, starting in the new school year. He asked me to stay for the spring since he already thinks we don't see each other enough."

I thought he'd already turned that down. "Didn't he decide to stay in Seattle for a few more years?"

Julie takes a sip of water. "Apparently, he had another meeting with their provost and changed his mind, so I guess you'll have me for the whole year."

I'm not sure how to feel about this news. I'd been trying to convince her to stay for months. I should probably be thrilled about this, but for some reason it doesn't seem right to celebrate. The waitress comes out with our food. I'm not as hungry all of a sudden.

Julie takes a bit of salad and says, "So, Ben, what else should I know about you?"

"I like to cook sometimes."

"What kind of food?"

"Nothing too fancy. Unless I have a visitor." He squeezes my leg under the table. "Oliver tells me you're an incredible writer."

"I don't know about *that*," she says, slightly embarrassed. "But I do write a lot. Mostly poetry these days. I'm in a creative writing class right now."

"I'm always jealous of creative people," Ben says. "All the ideas you come up with. I struggle writing birthday cards."

"Do you read a lot?"

"Not as much as I want to," he admits. "The last thing I read was *The Paper Menagerie* by Ken Liu. Honestly, I needed time to recover. It's the only book that's ever made me cry."

Julie leans into the table. "Oh my god. *I cried, too.*"

They continue talking about their favorite books. Julie offers to give him some recommendations, which is a good sign from her. Coincidentally, they've both studied French, and they go on about some film called *The Umbrellas of Cherbourg*, which apparently inspired *La La Land*. Meanwhile, I haven't seen either movie.

It's really nice to all sit together, watch them hit it off for the first time. I wonder if they're getting along a little *too* well. When they start talking in French, I have to interrupt them. *"By the way, I'm also here."*

We finish dinner with an ice cream sundae. Then Ben gets up to use the bathroom. Julie waits a beat before she leans in and whispers, *"I like him more than I thought I would."*

"I told you, he's great."

"He's also really cute. Now, tell me how you *really* met."

"You heard him. We met at the conference," I say.

"Oliver."

"Why is that so hard to believe?!"

Julie releases a frustrated breath. "Fine, don't tell me. I hope he visits you again though."

I had a feeling she would approve of Ben. I'm sure the flowers gave him some bonus points. Eventually, we all make our way outside. Ben and I have to get going soon. I'm taking him somewhere special tonight.

We park near the footpaths. Ben follows me onto the trails, through the shortcut in the trees. The mountain air smells of pine and fresh snow. In the spring, the ground is usually blooming with wildflowers. Now it's covered with twigs and leaves. "We're almost there," I say, guiding us deeper into the woods. I've only been here a few times before, but I know every step from memory. It's completely dark by the time we break through the trees.

An endless field stretches before us, touching the line of mountains in the distance. The dried barley cracks beneath my shoes. At least it's easier to walk through now.

"It's prettier in the spring," I admit.

Ben takes a few steps out, brushing his hair back. He looks around and says, "What do you mean? It's beautiful out here!"

I smile and take his hand. Then I lead him farther down the field. It doesn't even matter that the ground is cold—we lie down next to each other and stare up at the sky. The stars are so bright out here, illuminating everything around us. It always fees like another world out here. We're miles and miles from town.

"I've never seen the sky this clear before," Ben says, breathlessly. He turns his head, squeezing my hand. "I can see why you wanted to take me here."

"I knew you'd like it."

I run my fingers over his cold cheek, down to his warm lips. Then I lean forward to kiss him. I close my eyes, feeling his hand move across my neck. Then we untangle and cast our eyes upward, sharing the sky again. The constellations seem so close, like we could almost reach out and pull them down. "Feels like we're the only two people in the universe," Ben whispers.

"I was thinking the same thing."

"Maybe we entered a new timeline."

"Honestly, at this point, that wouldn't surprise me."

A silence passes. Then Ben looks at me again. "Do you think you'll ever go back? To your own timeline, I mean. I know we haven't talked about it yet."

"I don't know," I answer. "I have no idea why I'm still here. But it's been almost a week now. Maybe this is my new reality and I should just get used to it."

"This all must be weird for you. Having to experience everything a second time."

"It's not that bad." I take in a breath and let it out. "But the last few days have been confusing. I don't know if I should restudy for finals I've already taken. I'm actually worried I might fail a second time around." What I don't say out loud is that the worst part is that Mom is still not talking to me. I wish I could fix that somehow. I wish I could take back the stupid choices I made the other night.

"At least you'll have Julie now," Ben says.

"Yeah. I guess that's true."

"You must be happy she's staying. I know you really missed her while she was gone."

"I actually can't believe it." I look at him again. "Do you think that happened because of me? Maybe coming back changed something."

Ben considers this. "It's certainly possible. Some things are bound to be different, right? It's Newton's third law—for every action, there is an equal and opposite reaction. There's no way you can control everything."

"I guess you're right. But I still feel guilty about it. She was so happy studying abroad, you know? She would light up telling me about all of her experiences in Copenhagen."

"Well, *I'm* happier with you here," Ben says.

I smile at him. "I'm happy with *you*, too."

Who cares what timeline we're in. All that matters is we have each other. Maybe it was destined to be this way. Of course, there are still questions turning in my head. I look at Ben and ask, "Do you still think about how any of this is happening?"

"How could I not?" he answers.

"There has to be a reason for it, right? Why we found each other. Like, maybe there's some invisible string that connects us or something. No matter what timeline we're in."

"Not necessarily."

"Why not?"

"I don't really believe in things like that," he says, placing one arm behind his head. "That some people are destined to meet, if you know what I mean. What if you and I were just in the right place at the right time? I mean, isn't that *more* meaningful, if you actually think about it? Out of all the billions of people in the world, across all the different timelines, we chose each other. What's the probability of that?"

"I guess you're right," I say.

We look at each other. Then he leans forward to kiss me again. I wish I could freeze this moment so we could live in it forever. But time continues to move, despite everything else. And we can't stay out here all night.

"I hate that we both have class tomorrow," I say.

Ben sighs. "I know. I would skip if I hadn't just failed a quiz."

"You failed a quiz?"

"Yeah it's not like me, huh? I haven't been able to focus recently. I guess I fell behind more than I thought. Didn't realize how quickly it would catch up to me," he sighs. "Even worse, I forgot to turn in the fellowship application. Apparently, I mixed up the dates and missed the deadline yesterday."

"Wait, the one you've been talking about?"

Ben nods.

"But you won that—"

It slips out before I can catch myself. I checked last week, but I wasn't sure if I should tell him. How would I know he'd forget to turn it in?

Ben blinks at me. "What do you mean?"

I swallow my breath and say, "I looked it up recently. There was an article that said you won the fellowship."

"And you were hiding that from me?"

I don't know what to say. "No, I just wasn't sure if I should tell you or not. I mean, you said you liked surprises when we last talked about it. I didn't think this would happen."

He thinks about it. "I guess I did say that."

"I'm sorry," I say.

Ben sighs. "It's alright. It's my fault for falling behind."

That's not completely true. After all, he wouldn't have forgotten if it wasn't for me. "I feel like it's my fault though. For spending so much time distracting you."

Ben squeezes my hand again. "Don't say that. I'm here because I want to be here. I promise. I wouldn't change anything about these last few weeks."

"I still feel bad about it."

"It's not the end of the world. I can always apply next year."

The he kisses me on the cheek. I smile back at him, but I don't stop thinking about his fellowship. I think of the image of him in the article I found. Ben has worked so hard toward his future. Am I getting in the way of that?

A bright streak of light shoots across the sky.

Ben and I turn our heads to look. A few seconds later, another streak appears. Followed by another one. And another one. The next thing I know, there are hundreds of them illuminating the night sky.

"This looks insane," I say.

"I wonder what it's from."

"You mean, you don't know?"

"The Geminids meteor shower happens around this time of year," he says. "But I've never seen it like *this* before. It has to be something else."

I suddenly remember something. At the club fair, the girl

mentioned they were hosting a stargazing event for a rare meteor shower. "This must be Roy's Comet," I say.

"Roy's Comet? How do you know about that?"

"Someone from the astronomy club mentioned it last week. They invited me to come see it before it disappears. It's supposed to be gone for a while, right?"

"If I remember correctly, it's orbital period is twenty-nine years." The shower continues, casting blue lines across his face. "I think I remember reading about that . . . A chunk of it broke off, which would cause a larger meteor shower than expected. But that wouldn't happen until May."

"Right. Then this can't be it."

Ben stares at the sky again. "Wait a minute . . ." He pushes himself up a little. "That's weird. That looks like the Leo constellation."

"What's weird about that?"

"It should only be visible in the spring," he says, tilting his head a little. "And it shouldn't be next to Cepheus . . . It's like the skies have merged or something."

I push myself up for a better look. There *is* something slightly off about the stars. I can't put my finger on it though. "Are you saying you can see some constellations from the *spring*?"

"I don't really know what I'm seeing."

"So it could be Roy's Comet, then?"

"It shouldn't be, but honestly, nothing's making sense anymore."

We're both silent for a long time. Maybe this has something to do with what's happening between us. The reason our timelines are connected and why I can't go back. Streaks of light continue to burst through the sky as we lie in the fields.

CHAPTER TWENTY-THREE

"What are you doing back here?" Sam's voice echoes through the darkness.

I look around for him, but I can't see anything through the wall of mist. Only my two hands, reaching out into the emptiness. There's nothing to grasp—no shapes, no corners of a room, no sense of time. I wander around, hoping to catch his voice again. I can't tell how long I've been searching or what direction this is. The moment I think I've found him, everything fades like sand through my fingers. All that's left is a strange feeling in my chest. An understanding that no matter what direction I run, no matter how far, I'll never catch up to him.

The feeling stays with me even long after I wake up.

★ ★ ★

It's another cold December morning. My breath turns to clouds as I head to campus. It's been a full week since waking up in this timeline. I've come to accept that I might be here for good. I'm still trying to figure out my schedule. It would be easier if my phone was working right. I can't make any calls or open my apps without it glitching the entire screen. I'll have to get a new one soon. At least I can still send and receive messages. There's one from Ben.

> Morning

> Text me when you're awake

He's always up hours before me. We had such an incredible night beneath the stars. I can still feel his lips on mine, but there's a knot of guilt in my chest. I can't believe he missed the deadline for his fellowship application. It was so important to him. I can't stop blaming myself for it. He would have won it if it hadn't been for me, right? We're supposed to see each other again this weekend, but I know he's behind on work. I hate to think I might be for keeping him from accomplishing his goals. Maybe we should take some time apart. Give him a chance to catch up. As much as I love seeing Ben, all the traveling back and forth between our cities is exhausting. Especially with finals coming up. My head pounds just from thinking about it.

* * *

I have Math Modeling in an hour, but I don't feel like sitting through it again. It makes me miss my spring schedule, especially Professor Clarke's class. As confusing as she is sometimes, it was the only course I truly enjoyed. In a lot of ways, it was like a sanctuary from the world. It brought me a sense of comfort. I miss her interesting lectures. The questions she had us thinking about for weeks.

I decide to stop by her office. Maybe she'll be in today. I've never actually been there before, so when I get to the philosophy building, I search around, looking for the door with her name on it. Thankfully, the light is on. I knock on the door and poke my head in.

"Oliver? What a surprise."

"Hi, Professor Clarke."

"*Professor?*" she says, almost teasingly. "That's very formal of you. No need to call me that unless you're in one of my classes."

"Oh, right."

I haven't taken her spring class yet. I have to keep reminding myself that.

"To what do I owe the pleasure of seeing you? I hope Julie didn't send you to check up on me."

"No."

She gives me a suspicious look. "Did someone *else* send you to check up on me?"

"No, I just thought I'd stop and say hi."

"Oh." She relaxes, pointing to the chair in front of her desk. "Well then, please, come in and take seat."

It feels nice to see her again, sit down together. I scan the books on the shelves, written in different languages. There's a few photos on the wall. "I like your office," I tell her.

"Thank you." She leans back in her chair. "It usually gets more cluttered throughout the year. So you've caught me at a very good time."

"What are you teaching this quarter?"

"The Philosophy of the Mind," she answers. "It's one of my favorite courses to teach. Always fascinating to get students thinking about their own consciousness."

"That sound interesting," I say, nodding. "You know, I've been thinking about taking some philosophy classes."

"Oh? What inspired that?"

"I've just been interested in it lately. I read this one quote somewhere that made me think about myself." I pause to remember it. "It was something like, *the home is our first universe.*"

"Sounds like Bachelard." Professor Clarke nods knowingly. "It must mean something to you, if it's inspiring you to learn more. I'm curious what it's made you think about."

I stare at my hands and say, "To be honest, I didn't really get it at first. I'm sure you know I moved around a lot when I was young. I think that gave me a limited sense of what a home is, you know? But I'm learning it's more than the house you live in. It's something you make yourself. With the people you meet, the places you go." In a lot of ways, Ellensburg is my home, right? It's where I've lived my entire life. It's also all that I really know. I don't understand much of the world beyond it. I'm starting to realize I don't understand a lot of things.

Professor Clarke laces her fingers together. "I'm glad it resonated with you. You might have enjoyed the class I'm teaching."

"I wish I'd known about it sooner," I say. "But I'm looking forward to taking your class in the spring."

Professor Clarke frowns. "Unfortunately, I might not be

teaching it in the spring."

"Why not?"

"There are a few factors." She picks up the stack of papers and sets them behind her. "It's an additional course I take on every so often. Now that Julie is staying for the spring, I might need to cancel as I won't have the time."

"So when will you teach it then?"

"Not for a while. I'll be on sabbatical next year, so likely when I return."

I was just sitting in her class. I haven't even finished reading *The Poetics of Space*. How could she not be teaching it? I must have gone quiet for too long, because Professor Clarke says, "Is something else bothering you, Oliver?"

I stare at my hands again. I should just tell her I'm fine, but she'd probably sense that's not the truth. I remember something she said in class. *Time is always in motion*. I wonder what she would think about this strange situation I'm in. I look up and say, "Can I ask you something else? It might be an odd question."

"Please."

There's a brief silence as I think about how to word this. "Do you believe in alternate universes?"

"I have no reason not to," she says.

"Is that a *yes*?"

"It's most certainly not a *no*."

I lean forward, hoping she'll say more.

"You're not the first to ask this question," she continues. "Whether or not other versions of our world exist. There are endless theories out there, if that's what you're looking for. Simulations, bubble theory, string theory. Every field from philosophy to quantum physics has danced with the possibility. Of course, there's nothing to prove any of it. But there's also nothing to disprove it, either."

"So what you're saying is, there are a lot of people who believe it. But no one actually knows anything," I gather.

"What I'm saying is, there are a lot of people who are, at least, open to the *possibility* of their existence," she clarifies. "The universe is filled with endless paradoxes and contradictions that no one can explain away. Even the most fundamental laws that hold together everything we know to be true have been broken at one point or another. So maybe it's not so crazy to believe that alternate universes exist all around us. Even if you can't see it."

"You think there are infinite versions of us out there?"

"I think there are infinite possibilities of how we live our lives." She gestures expressively. "Different timelines of *what-ifs* branching out like tiny bubbles from a champagne fountain. Maybe from every seemingly inconsequential decision we make."

It's hard to imagine *infinite* versions of me. Me here. Me still in spring. Maybe there's a universe where Ben didn't pick up the phone and we never met. "Do you think we have any choice at all? As in, which universe we end up in. Sorry if that's a stupid question."

"That's not stupid at all. Of course, I don't know the answer." She pauses to think about it. "It's more like *time* in that way. We're all limited by our perception of it. Maybe it's something that *stretches* and compacts and flows with no end or beginning. We may never be able to change time, but we can change the way we understand ourselves in it. It just takes a bit of reorienting."

"I'm not exactly sure what that means," I admit.

"Think about the way we lose track of time," she continues. "It is a very *real* feeling that we all experience, isn't it? Like when we forget to look at the clock to count how many minutes have passed. You see, we've been taught to check things off schedules, to think of time as something that is always running out, which in turn forces us to live ahead of ourselves. In order to change the way we think about it, we have to understand how it tangles itself around every part of our lives in different ways. Only when we stop trying to pin it down does time begin to move in another direction."

There's so much to process. I'm not sure how much of it relates to me because I haven't been living ahead of myself. If anything, I've been trying to stop time from moving at all. To keep things the way they are for just a little bit longer. Now I'm reliving the last six months of my life. I wonder what Professor Clarke would think if she knew. I wish we could talk for another hour, for many more hours, but there's a knock on the door. Another student is here to see her, so I get up from the chair and say goodbye.

"Stop by anytime," she says. "I mean that."

I smile. "Thank you. I definitely will."

I should probably get some studying done before class, but all I can think about are the other versions of me branching out in different timelines. How do I know if I'm living in the right one? I can't believe Professor Clarke isn't teaching her spring class. And that Julie won't be studying abroad anymore. What else might have changed?

I check my phone on the way to the library. There's a

message from Ben.

> I was reading about Roy's Comet. It became visible in July

> Which is around the time I first received your messages

I pause to take this in.

> That's weird

> Do you think it means anything?

> I'm not sure. It's probably a coincidence

> I figure the comet's gone by now

> It's actually still visible

> But should be gone by tonight

I'm not sure what to make of this. I know Ben believes in coincidences more than fate. But what if all these things *are* connected somehow? Me getting stuck here at the same time the comet is disappearing. Maybe there was a ripple in space-time or something, causing our worlds to flow into each other. I know I'm just making stuff up right now. I shouldn't be thinking about this anyway. I should be happy about being in the timeline with Ben.

But why does it feel like I don't belong here? I mean, it's

not like it's going particularly well so far. I already messed up a few things, includes ruining Mom's birthday. I think about what's been happening with Ben, too. I wonder if being together isn't actually what's best for him right now. I know he doesn't blame me for losing the fellowship, but I still blame myself for it. He'd never failed a quiz until he started spending time with me. I'm the common factor across all this.

Ben's the greatest thing to happen to me in a long time, but I would never want to hold him back from anything. Especially when I don't have my own life figured out. I care about him way too much. I've never felt this stuck before. I think again about the other versions of me. If there really *are* an infinite number of possibilities out there, maybe there's one where I find my way back.

CHAPTER TWENTY-FOUR

"Only when we stop trying to pin it down does time begin to move in another direction."

Professor Clarke's words keep turning in my head. I'm still not sure how this idea is supposed to help me right now. Especially when I don't really understand it. What does it even mean for "time to move in another direction"? All I want is for things to go back to the way they were. To wake up in my dorm room again. To still be able to visit Ben whenever I wanted. I wish he was here with me now.

I wonder what Julie would think about everything. It's annoying that I can't talk with her about this. I don't know why I've kept it a secret for so long. Probably because I wouldn't believe it myself if someone else told me this story.

I stare at the phone for a moment. Maybe it's time to finally tell her.

YOU'VE FOUND OLIVER

> Julie

> Where are you

It takes a minute for her to respond.

> Home why?

> Ok don't go anywhere! I'm coming over

I turn around and make my way to Julie's house. She lives about twenty-five minutes from campus. I take my usual shortcut through the neighborhood. I remember the first time I visited her. It was a few weeks after Sam died. We weren't even friends at the time, but I really needed someone to talk to. So I threw rocks at her window until she came outside. I feel those nerves returning while I wait for her to open the front door.

"Hey," she says.

"Hi. Can we chat?"

"Oh . . . sure."

I go inside, and she closes the door behind me. It's been a minute since I've been here. I used to pop in all the time, before she went abroad. Her hallway is filled with pictures of her growing up in Seattle. I take off my shoes and follow her into the living room.

"Don't you have class today?" she asks.

"I'm not really thinking about school right now."

"Oh. Everything okay?"

"Yeah. I mean, sort of. Well, not exactly. It's hard to explain—"

"Oliver, just spit it out."

I realize I'm pacing around a little. So I collect myself and say, "You might want to sit down for this, okay?"

"Alright. But you're scaring me a little."

Julie takes a seat on the sofa and waits for me to continue. I'm not really sure where to start. Maybe this isn't even a good idea. Then I remember one of our last phone calls. When I asked her, *"If I told you something crazy, would you believe me?"* And her answer was, *"You can tell me anything. No matter what it is."*

I hold on to that promise as I look at her and say, "Do you know how I've been acting a little 'off' lately?"

"That's putting it mildly, but yes."

"There's a good reason for that, but you might not believe me when I tell you." The next words come out slowly. "I don't really know how to say this . . . but something strange happened to me recently . . . and now I'm living in the past."

"What are you talking about?"

"I know this sounds ridiculous, okay? But I really need you to believe me. Somehow I've entered a different timeline. It's supposed to be six month from now for me. I have no idea how this happened."

"I'm assuming this is some kind of prank," she says.

"This isn't a *prank*," I tell her. "Listen to me, okay? I'm supposed to be living in the spring. I've experienced all of this already."

She gives me a look. "Oliver . . . that's crazy."

"I *know* it sounds crazy, alright? But I'm being completely serious." I take a breath and try not to sound exasperated. "I'm telling you, *it's supposed to be spring*. I've already taken these classes. You already left to study abroad. I helped you pack your things! I'm taking your mom's class right now. We're reading this book called *The Poetics of Space*."

"Are you sure this wasn't a dream—"

"*It wasn't a dream.* Ben believes me! He's the only person I've told. We've known for weeks. I don't know how else to convince you."

"You're *sure* this isn't some prank?" she asks again.

I grasp her shoulders. "I swear on my life, my mom's life, everything."

Julie takes this in for a moment. "So what you're saying is you're actually from six months in the future?"

"*Yes.*"

A long silence passes between us. I'm not sure what else I can do to prove this. I hold my breath, waiting for her to throw a dozen questions at me, but Julie remains calm when she finally says, "Alright. So, what now?"

I blink at her. "So you actually believe me?"

"Yes." She rises from the couch. "*Unless this really is a prank—*"

I sit her down again and say, "I promise, it's not. I was just worried you wouldn't believe me. That's why I took so long to tell you."

Julie sighs. "Oliver. *Strange things happen all the time*, okay? Now explain to me what exactly is going on. How did this happen?"

I feel some weight lifted off my shoulders. "It started a few weeks ago. I was going back and forth for a while, which I didn't realize at first. But I think I'm stuck here now, so I'm sort of freaking out a little. I don't know how to get back."

"So it's been *weeks*?"

"*Yes*, ever since I started seeing Ben."

"Does he have something to do with this? I'm confused."

I should start from the beginning. I take another deep breath. "This is embarrassing, but I was texting Sam's old number for a while after he died. I didn't realize it had already transferred to someone else. And one day, when I accidently called it, Ben picked up the phone."

"So that's how you guys actually know each other?"

I nod. "Yeah."

"You called Sam's number . . ."

I explain the different timelines. Moving between them every time Ben and I met up. The moments we realized something was off: the bakery, the cherry blossoms, seeing her outside the library. "I probably should have noticed it sooner," I admit.

She rubs her temples, processing this. "I guess that part makes more sense looking back. I remember you showed up with Ben, saying how much you needed to talk. And the next day you didn't remember that at all. I should have guessed something was up."

I always wondered what happens after I leave. "It's alright. Honestly, I didn't really mind at first. But I think I'm stuck here now."

"How do you know that?"

"Because I always woke up to my own timeline," I explain. "But it's been over a week now. I don't understand what I'm still doing here."

"So you want to go back?"

"I'm not really sure, but I don't want to regret not trying, you know?" My answer might have been different a few days ago. But it's starting to feel like I'm living a different life. Like this one doesn't truly belong to me.

"I'm still really confused," she says, pressing her lips together. "This is all so . . . What do you think caused this?"

"I don't know," I say, exasperated. "I noticed that things were different when Ben and I were together. I would always slip into his timeline. The one we're in now. The first time we met up, I actually couldn't find him at first, even though he said he was standing at the same spot. Then I called him, and the next thing I knew, he was right there."

Julie looks at me. "So you think it's Sam's phone number?"

"It must have something to do with it." After all, it's what connected us from the beginning.

"What happens if you call it now?"

"My phone's not working, so I can't call *anyone*." I take it out of my pocket to show her.

"Did you drop it or something? What if that's the reason?"

"I don't remember doing that," I say, checking the edges. "It just started glitching on me recently. I've restarted it a hundred times."

Julie checks the phone herself. Of course, it doesn't work for her, either. She stares at it for a long moment. Then she rises from the couch and says, "I might have an idea. Hold on."

I wait in the living room while she heads upstairs. A moment later, she comes back down, holding a small plastic bag close to her chest. She sits on the couch and hands it to me silently.

"What's this?" I ask.

"Some of Sam's things."

I don't know what to say at first. Then I open the bag slowly. There are a few things inside, including his old cell phone. I take it out, looking at it more closely. "Julie, where did you get this?"

"I might have broken into his house at one point. But we don't need to talk about that now."

It feels weird holding it in my hands again. "What are you giving it to me for?"

"Why don't you try to use it," she says.

"Really?"

"I'm sure he wouldn't mind. Just replace the SIM card."

I stare at my reflection in the screen. Then I remove the SIM card from my phone and place it in Sam's. It takes a while for the phone to set up. I try opening a few applications once it finishes, but it has the same problems as before. "This isn't working, either. Maybe it's my SIM card or something."

"That's weird. Let me see it." Julie tries to call herself, but the screen glitches again. She tries a few times before handing it back to me. "Yeah, I don't know why it's not working."

"Me neither."

At least my messages are all there. I run my hand along the screen. I can't believe I'm holding his phone again. I'm about to switch back to my own when I notice something . . .

The month on the screen is different.

"Wait a second. Look at the date—"

I hand the phone back to Julie.

She squints at the screen. "Why does it say April twenty-ninth?"

"That's what day's it's supposed to be! For me!"

"So . . . what does that mean?"

"I don't really know, to be honest. But it has to mean *something*, right?" Maybe the timelines are connected again. Does that mean I'll be able to return to my own?

"It could be a good sign," Julie says.

"I hope so."

"How do you normally get back again?"

"It usually just happens after I fall asleep."

Julie stares at the screen. Then she hands back the phone and says, "I guess you'll find out later, then."

"I hope it works this time."

"If you wake up in the future tomorrow, will you ever return to this timeline again?"

I look at her. "I don't know," I admit.

I hadn't really thought of that before. I stare at the date on my phone again. Does that mean this could be my last day here? Maybe I should think this through some more, but this might be my only chance to go back. What does it mean for me and Ben . . .

Will we ever be able to see each other again?

Eventually, I rise back up. "I have to go to Seattle . . ."

"For what?"

"I need to see Ben."

"You mean, right now?"

Maybe I'm overthinking this. There's a chance nothing will change at all. But I don't want to regret leaving without saying goodbye. Who knows how long it will be before we see each other again. *If* we see each other again. I pace the room for a second, wondering if I should take the bus. Thankfully, Julie says I can borrow her mom's car. I just have to bring it back tonight. She hands me the keys and places my old phone in the bag of Sam's things.

"There should be a car charger in there, too."

We hug each other before I head out the door, and I remember something. I turn around and take her by the shoulders. "I forgot to mention this. Just in case I don't see you again in this timeline. You need to go to the program in Copenhagen. Trust me, you'll love it there. Promise me, okay?"

"I'll keep that in mind," she says.

"I'm serious, Julie."

"*Okay.*"

I give her another hug, then head out to the car. As I'm about to drive off, Julie has come outside for some reason. I roll down the window.

"I wanted to say this really quick," she starts. "No matter which timeline you end up in, there's something important I want to tell you later. Just remember to ask me, okay?"

"What's it about?"

"Don't worry about that now. Just ask me later. I'll know what you mean."

"Okay."

I wonder what she has to tell me, but I should really get going. I turn onto the street as Julie waves goodbye from the driveway.

CHAPTER TWENTY-FIVE

Somewhere in another universe, Ben and I are lying in the field together. The sun is shining overhead as the grass rolls around us like ocean waves. There are no classes, seasons, or highways that separate us. Only a few centimeters of mountain air as his arm gently brushes mine. Time doesn't really move in this universe, allowing us to lie there forever, staring up at the clouds. I wish I could somehow wake up to that one.

It's a two-hour drive to Seattle. Hopefully there's not much traffic on the way. I sent Ben a message beforehand. He should see it by the time I arrive. Sam's phone has one percent battery left. I take out the charger Julie gave me and plug it in.

There are a few other things inside the plastic bag, including a burned CD. Haven't touched one of these in a while. There's something written on it. *Sam & Ollie's Graduation Playlist*. For a second, I wonder if I misread. Was this found inside his car with the rest of his things?

Sam must have made it for our road trip to the senior bonfire, but I don't remember listening to it before. We were always arguing about the music. I probably convinced him to play something of mine instead. Luckily, the car actually has a CD player, so I put it inside and turn up the volume.

The first song opens with a strong set of drums. "Bed of Roses" by the Screaming Trees. One of Sam's favorite bands of all time. I imagine him tapping away at the dashboard with his fingers. I let the music play as I drive along the highway. I haven't heard these songs in ages. Fleetwood Mac, Elton John, Air Supply. Each one brings back a different memory. Almost like a hand on my shoulder, asking me to look back in time. For a moment, it feels like he's sitting in the car beside me.

My mind flashes back to that day. The two of us driving along this same road with the windows rolled halfway down . . . Sam is wearing his corduroy blue jacket. He looks at me from the passenger seat and says, "If you keep going this slow, we won't get there for"—he pretends to check his watch—"three and a half business days."

"Listen, Sam." I squeeze the steering wheel. "If you wanted to drive, you should have said something before we left, okay?"

"How was I supposed to know you were gonna go forty in a *sixty*?" He gestures at the speed limit sign that we're conveniently passing at just the right moment.

"First of all, I'm going forty-five. Secondly, I'm sorry if I want to keep everyone safe."

"Oliver, we're the only two people on the road."

"There are signs for *deer crossing*."

Sam folds his arms across his chest. "Fine, we'll be late for the deer."

"Thank you for understanding. Now roll up the window, it's getting cold."

"Okay, Mom."

"Don't call me that."

Sam laughs as I focus on my driving. The music continues on low volume. It's been a while since we've had some time to ourselves. Sam stares out the window for a moment. "Do you know what I've been thinking about a lot?" He turns back to look at me. "How much everything is going to change. After we graduate, I mean. Do you think about that, too?"

"I guess so? I'm sure some things will change. I don't know about everything though." After all, we'll still be living in Ellensburg. Central Washington is only a stone's throw from our high school.

"I feel like a lot of people are leaving this year," Sam says. "Even Spencer's going to Pullman. And you know Julie wants to leave."

I roll my eyes. "Well, let's be honest. She never liked it here." Frankly, I'm surprised she never moved back to Seattle to live with her dad. I'm sure Sam was probably the reason for that.

"I'm gonna go with her."

"As in like, to visit?"

"No. I'm moving with her."

"What are you talking about?"

"I was thinking of taking a year off," he says. "Maybe even

two. There are a lot more opportunities for me in Portland. And you don't really need a degree to pursue a music career."

"And when did you decide this?"

"A few months ago. Julie and I have talked about it a lot. But nothing's concrete yet. We're still waiting for her to hear back from Reed."

"I thought we were going to Central together." I don't know what else to say. We planned this years ago. I can't believe he's throwing this out of left field.

"That was our default. Everyone just goes there," he says, shrugging. "Maybe we should think beyond it, right? I mean, what's keeping us here anyway? Besides our families and stuff. I know we planned to stay for college, but maybe we're meant to do something else."

I say nothing.

"I hope you're not mad. You don't have to stay, either, you know?"

I scoff. "And where would I go?"

"Maybe you should think about it," Sam says. "Life's too short to stay in one place, waiting for things to happen. But I get it though. Going to the same places, seeing the same people. There's something nice about that. I don't want to wake up one day and feel like I'm not living the life I'm supposed to live. Just because staying here was more comfortable. Sometimes, you need to take that risk." He lets me take this in. "You know what they say. We can't stay in the past forever."

Sam's words echo through me.

I wish you got the chance to go. I wish you got the chance to live out that life.

✱ ✱ ✱

A car zooms past my window, pulling me back to myself. I turn my head and glance at the empty passenger seat. For a moment, it felt like Sam was actually there. I wasn't expecting to be hit with this vivid memory. Maybe this music is too much for right now.

I'm about to take out the CD when a new song comes on, filling the car with a familiar guitar. It takes me a few seconds to recognize it. "Both Sides Now" by Joni Mitchell. My body goes still for a second. It's one of Ben's favorite songs. I'd forgotten that he and Sam had this in common. Tears are forming in my eyes, but I hold them back and keep my eyes on the road. Joni Mitchell's voice rings through me. I never realized how beautiful the lyrics are.

It's life's illusions I recall
I really don't know life at all

I think about the first night Ben and I spent together. We were lying on his bed, listening to this song play from the living room. I remember falling asleep, wishing we could wake up next to each other. Now here I am, living in his timeline. These past few weeks have brought us so much closer. I don't want to imagine a world without Ben in it. Maybe I should just stay here so we can be together. After all, I've already lost someone I love. I don't want to lose him, too.

But what would our future look like? He already lost his fellowship because of me, even though he won't admit that to himself. Who knows what other opportunities he might miss. I don't want to hold him back from accomplishing his dreams. Not to mention, I'm now doing worse in my classes, too. I'm skipping another one right now to go see him. I think back to the article I found about Ben winning the fellowship. I want him to be the best version of himself. Maybe that doesn't include me. At least, not right now anyway.

I cross the bridge into Seattle. The sun burns low over the familiar skyline as I drive into the city. Ben just texted me back. He should be out of office hours soon. We're going to meet somewhere on campus. I find an empty spot on the street and park the car. There's another message from him.

> Are you here?

> I'm at the department building

> Just parked the car. I can meet you there

I slide my hands in my pockets and cut through the quad. My breath fogs as I move through the crowd of students in winter coats. I've been here enough times to know my way there without directions. As the redbrick building comes into view, someone calls my name from above.

"Oliver."

Ben smiles down at me from the roof. I smile and wave back at him. Then I head inside and press the button for the elevator. We were just stargazing last night. I wasn't expecting to see him again this soon. When I get to the roof, Ben is adjusting a telescope that's angled toward the sky. His face lights up the second he turns around. I kiss his lips and say, "Sorry for the surprise visit."

"What are you apologizing for? You know I like surprises."

I smile again. Then I glance at the telescope. "What's all this for?"

"I'm actually glad you came. I wanted to show you something." Ben brushes back his hair and checks the eyepiece. "I was trying to find Roy's Comet again, but it's a little too bright right now."

I think back to last night. "Is the sky still looking weird?"

"Not that I can tell," he says.

I wonder what that could mean. Maybe the other timeline really is closing. "I might have figured out how to go back," I tell him.

Ben looks at me. "Really? How?"

"I'm actually not completely sure," I admit. "There was something wrong with my phone before, but I finally switched to a different one. Look at the date on the screen." I hand over the phone to him.

Ben reads the screen. "It says April."

"My old phone never showed that before."

"Interesting. Maybe that means it's still connected somehow."

"I guess we'll find out soon." I swallow my breath. "To be honest, I'm a little scared about it."

"Scared of what?"

"Losing you."

"Why would you lose me?"

A cold breeze blows across the rooftop. I almost don't want to say it out loud. "What if the connection closes this time and we can't see each other again . . ."

Ben takes this in for a moment. "I would be lying if I said I hadn't thought about this," he says in a soft voice. "That this could all end at some point, given how impossible it seemed to begin with. For a while, I wondered if I would stop hearing from you one day. I thought this might be temporary, like most other things in the world. When I woke up that one morning and realized you were still here, I thought maybe we could actually make this work. That we could stay together and just be happy." He touches my face. "But I don't want to make you stay. Especially if you want to go back."

I've thought about this a million times, too. "It's not exactly that I want to go back. But I think I need to. And maybe those two things aren't always the same." I take his hands in mine. His eyes are beautiful in the golden light. "Listen, Ben. I wish I could spend every second with you, but I've also seen what your life looks like without me in it. You deserve the world. I don't want to get in the way of that."

"You're not getting in the way," he says.

"We both know that's not completely true. You're the best thing to happen to me in a long time, but I think we each need to focus on ourselves for the moment." I smile at him. "Who knows, maybe we'll get another chance at this later on."

"And what if we don't?"

"Then I'll search every universe to find you." I lean forward, pressing my lips against his. His hands are warm around my neck. The sun continues to fade, casting shadows on the roof. Unfortunately, I can't stay for too long. I pull away and say, "I have to get back home soon."

"But you just got here," Ben says.

"I know, but there's something important I need to fix."

The light in his eyes dims. "This could be the last time I see you . . ."

There's a chance nothing will happen at all, so maybe we're worrying for no reason. But I have to say goodbye just in case. That's the reason I came here. I don't want to wake up in the morning and regret leaving without seeing him one more time.

I take his hands, lace our fingers together. "Remember what you said yesterday, about the probability of us choosing each other from all the timelines out there? I think that is beautiful, but I think I'm right, too. That we will always be connected somehow. And if that's true, maybe we'll find each other again."

"Maybe you're right about that," he says.

I kiss Ben longer, as if it's our last time. I hope I'm not making a mistake. Why would the universe connect us just to have us say goodbye in the end? Hopefully, this won't be the end of our story.

I wish I could stay with him longer, but there's someone else I need to see before I go.

CHAPTER TWENTY-SIX

I've made some mistakes in this timeline. But there's one I *have* to fix before going back.

I'm still mad at myself for ditching Mom's birthday. I keep thinking about her sitting in the ceramics class, waiting for me to show up. I can't believe I lost that memory just to go to Nolan's stupid party. We haven't had a chance to talk about it. Hopefully, there's still time to make things right. She's the most important person in my life. The last thing I would ever want is to leave things this way.

Once I get back to Ellensburg, I still have a few hours before everything closes. I make a quick stop in town and then drive to Julie's to drop off the car before hurrying home. I manage to clean up a little before Mom finally comes through the door.

"*Surprise*," I say.

The birthday candle flickers in the air between us. Mom blinks at the plate in my hands, looking confused. When I stopped by the bakery earlier, they had one slice of her favorite caramel coconut cake left. I hold it out for her. "Go on. Make a wish."

"You know it isn't my birthday," she says.

I had a feeling she would still be upset. I let out a breath and say, "I know. I'm sorry. I should have been there last week. I'm the worst son in the world. Please let me make up for it, okay?"

Mom gives me a long look. For a second, I think she might walk away, but she blows out her candle instead. We smile at each other. There's no time to take a bite though.

"Keep your jacket on. We have to leave right now."

"Where are we going—" she starts.

I set down the plate and pull her out the door, letting her know it's a surprise. It's a short drive to the ceramics studio. Julie was kind enough to call them for me while I was on my way back from Seattle. Their last class of the day ended half an hour ago. Apparently, the woman said no at first. But when Julie told her the story, she remembered my mom from the week before. She's allowing us to come to the studio for the next hour, while she's cleaning up.

It's nice being the only two people here, almost like we rented the place for ourselves. I help Mom make her plate and place it in the kiln. Of course, she decides to paint it the same green as my eyes. Just like the one she made before, in the other timeline. She looks just as happy as she did the first time we came here.

"This was what I wished for," she whispers to me.

I can't help but smile. I know this isn't exactly like before, but I'm glad I was able to do this with her. I really hope this brings us closer again. Later at home, Mom and I split the slice of cake and put a frozen pizza in the oven. We watch an episode of her favorite show before she heads off to bed.

It's late when I finally lie down on the sofa. I'm tired from the hours of driving today. I'm not sure where I'll wake up in the morning. My eyelids feel heavy as I check my phone. The date hasn't changed since the last time I checked—it's still April. But there's a few new text messages from Ben. I open our conversation right away.

> Hope you made it back safe

> Wish we had a little more time together though. I regret not kissing you longer. And not holding you in my arms for a few more seconds. I thought about what you said. That you and I are connected somehow. Maybe we were always supposed to meet each other. Regardless of what universe we were in. It makes it more painful to think about you leaving

> I hope you're right about everything. That this isn't the last time I'll see you. Who knows. Maybe the stars will align differently next time. So we can truly be together. I'll wish for that more than anything in the world. But if for some reason it doesn't happen, I want you to know I'm glad you came into my life. That I won't forget about us no matter what happens

> Missing you already. Hopefully you get back to where you need

I read the message over again. I'm not sure if he's still awake, but I write him a response.

> Sorry I had to leave so quickly

> I wish we had more time together too. I wish a lot of things could be different. I wish I was with you right now. So I can kiss you again. And we could fall asleep together. Out of all the universes I could have ended up in, I'm grateful it was yours

> I'm also happy you came into my life. That we got to know each other more these past few weeks. Just because our time might be temporary, it doesn't mean my connection to you is. We're a part of each other now. No matter what timelines we end up in. I'm not sure what will happen tomorrow. Maybe nothing will change at all. But in case I don't come back, I want you to know something

> I love you

> I wish I had told you in person

I've never liked the word *goodbye,* so I don't say it this time. I just keep the phone next to me as I close my eyes. I hope he gets the message. The rest of the world fades around me as I fall asleep.

CHAPTER TWENTY-SEVEN

Millions of light years away, two giant black holes have fallen in love. As they move closer together, they become locked in a celestial dance, creating invisible waves that spread throughout the universe. Their love is so powerful that, for a brief moment, they outshine everything else in the cosmos as they merge together to become one. Their energy travels for all of eternity, sending ripples across time and space, distorting the fabric of reality itself.

For as long as I can remember, I've always thought of time as a string of pearls. A collection of individual moments connected in a perfect, chronological order that begins in the past. But maybe the past doesn't actually move farther away as you move through time. Maybe memories are not pearls at all, but stars scattered across the universe, some shining more brightly than others, creating constellations that we get to map for ourselves.

I imagine different versions of me out there, drawing different constellations. Maybe some of them connect at certain points, crossing into each other as time stretches and flows around us.

* * *

When I wake up in the morning, something has changed. Sunlight bounces like water on the ceiling. I lie there for a moment, allowing my eyes to adjust themselves. Then the world comes into focus.

Plaid sheets. A stack of books against the wall. A curtain that divides the room in half.

I'm in my dorm again. That means I've made it back to my own timeline. I blink a few times, to make sure I'm not dreaming. Then I push myself up and take in the rest of the room. I don't have to look outside to know it's spring. I can smell the flowers and freshly cut grass from the opened window.

Then I remember Ben.

I search for my phone. He usually texts me first thing in the morning. There are a couple text notifications. But none of them are from him. Maybe he's still sleeping. I have to tell him I made it back to home.

But something is wrong. All my messages with him are gone. Did I delete them all by accident? For a moment, I think my phone is still broken, but everything else seems to be working fine again.

As I'm searching for them, I notice something else. Ben's name isn't in my contacts. What happened to our conversations these past few months? All I can find are the old messages I sent to Sam. I try sending a message anyway, but it doesn't seem to go through. What happened? How am I supposed to reach him now?

My mind goes back to last night. I knew there was a chance we might not see each other again, but I hoped our messages would still work. I thought maybe we could still text each other.

Does this mean our connection has ended for good?

I don't even know if he read my message from last night. I stare at the phone for a long moment. Maybe this is only a temporary glitch? I send him a few more messages hoping they go through eventually.

But nothing changes the next day. Or the day after that. I wish I could wait around for him. Time continues to move forward. I return to my spring classes. Everything appears to be normal again. It takes a few days to adjust to my schedule, but I manage to turn in my final papers on time. To my surprise, I do a little better than I expected. That's likely because of all the time I've had to myself lately. I'm particularly proud of the feedback I received from Professor Clarke. I'm already planning to take more of her classes. She even says I could be one of her TAs next year.

The cherry blossoms are all gone, signaling the end of the season. I keep hoping to wake up to a text from Ben. Any sign from the universe, letting me know he's trying to reach me, too. There's nothing but the memories of the last few months.

Just when I'm starting to believe it was all a dream, I find some of his things in my room. The pen he stole from the diner. His brown jacket that I never returned. This means it was all real. I couldn't have imagined everything, right?

But the days turn into weeks. Then a few months go by without a word from Ben. Once in a while, I'll send him another message.

> I miss you
>
> I hope everything's well
>
> How long will it be until I hear from you?

Sometimes, I wonder if I made a mistake. Then I imagine him living his life to the fullest, achieving everything that was meant for him. I hope he reapplied to the fellowship he wanted.

I'm doing better myself these days. I know I don't need to have everything figured out yet, but I joined a few clubs at school, including ultimate frisbee, which Rami recommended for making new friends. I'm also leaning toward majoring in philosophy. In a lot of ways, Ben inspired that. He was pursuing something he truly loved. Sometimes, I wish I could tell him about everything. Update him on how my life is going. I'm sure he would be proud of me, too.

Eventually, Julie returns home for the summer. We spend the days catching up on everything. Maybe it's all in my head, but she has a certain glow now. Her hair is lighter, and she's nearly finished writing her book. Apparently, she has a character named after me. Being away from Ellensburg was truly the best decision for her. She's made several new friends who I got to meet over video call. We take a weekend trip to the coast before she goes off to Reed. Thankfully, it's only a few hours away from here, so we can visit each other often.

Not a day goes by that I don't think of Ben. Occasionally, I look up him up online. He's still not active on social media, so there's not much to find. Only the same articles that I've read before. Sometimes, I wonder if this version of him would recognize me. Aren't we connected in some cosmic way? I'm sure he would have reached out by now if that was true.

Every now and then, I take the bus to Seattle for the afternoon. I walk around the busy streets, hoping to bump into him. I even stop by all his favorite places, including the park near his apartment. Maybe I'll find him reading on the bench and we'll strike up a conversation. But I never see him. It's possible he doesn't even live there anymore.

I still glance at my phone, always hoping to see a message from him. As more time passes, I realize they're never coming. So I eventually stop waiting for them.

Of course, it doesn't mean I forget about him. The memories I keep of us feel like yesterday. I hope he knows how strong my love is. I would search the universe, across different timelines, just to catch another glimpse of him.

Sometimes, I feel sad about losing him. Then I remember how lucky we are. Of all the infinite possibilities out there, we chose each other. Maybe our time together was shorter than we both wanted, but I am forever changed by it. Everywhere I go, I find more reasons to miss him.

I miss him when I listen to music and one of our songs come on. I miss him when someone calls my name and, for a split second, I think it could be him. I miss him when I'm walking alone through town and pass the bakery that closed down. And I miss him every time I look up and see the stars freckled across the night sky. There's a quote from *The Poetics of Space* that sticks with me. Professor Clarke wrote it on the board on the last day of class.

"It is better to live in a state of impermanence than in one of finality." —Gaston Bachelard

I've been thinking about this more lately, especially as I look back on my life. As much as we want to, we can't control time or keep it from moving forward. Sometimes, we have to embrace the changes that come with it. Maybe there's something beautiful about that, living with the uncertainty of what's to come. You never know what possibilities will be born out of it.

But some things will always be certain. Like the sun rising in the morning. Or the leaves falling in the autumn and the cherry blossoms returning in the spring. *That he and I will always be connected.* And who knows? Maybe we'll see each other again in twenty-nine years, when the comet passes once more, sending streaks of light across the sky.

I hope he still remembers me then.

EPILOGUE

ONE AND A HALF YEARS LATER

It's early summer on a warm, sundrenched afternoon in a new city. Petals fall like snow into the canals that run between the narrow streets. I'm studying at the University of Amsterdam before the start of my junior year. It's my first time traveling to another country. Vibrant brick buildings lean into each other as houseboats float along the water. I was planning to work at Mr. Lee's bookstore for the summer, but Julie encouraged me to do something more adventurous. Expand my perspective of the world. So I looked into different study abroad programs.

Professor Clarke connected me to one of her colleagues here. He teaches a seminar on Greek philosophy, which I've been more interested in lately. He gave me a list of books to read on my own. I've been living here for over two weeks now. I bought a used bicycle the day after I arrived and have been riding it everywhere. It's a big part of the culture here. It's such an easy way to move through the city, feeling the summer breeze against your face.

It's strange to be thousands of miles away from home. Sometimes, I find myself biking for hours, crossing one bridge after another, discovering new parts of the city. But I make sure to stop every once in a while to explore things on foot. Mom asked me to send pictures of everything.

I get off my bike at The Nine Streets. It's a charming neighborhood, filled with little shops and restaurants that sit along the water. It's one of my favorite places to wander around after classes. There's this funny restaurant that sells hamburgers through a wall like a vending machine. I restrain myself from buying another cheese croquette, which has become a new obsession of mine. Instead, I grab a water and continue along the bustling street.

Amsterdam is crowded in the summertime. I wasn't sure if I would like it here at first. Especially having to be on my own for three months. There are so many things I haven't done yet, like visit the Anne Frank House or walk through the Van Gogh Museum, lay a blanket in the park and drink some wine with friends I haven't made yet. I'm looking forward to my first pride festival in July.

There's another reason I chose to come to Amsterdam, but I wasn't expecting to run into him so soon. . . .

I've turned down a quiet street I haven't visited before. Maybe it's the golden hour, but everything seems bathed in fairy light. He's sitting outside a café, reading a book. I almost didn't recognize him at first. Then I catch a glimpse of his face and go completely still. He's wearing a faded burgundy shirt, and his hair is cut shorter than I remember.

For a moment, all the timelines are connected again. I can't tell if this is another daydream. I knew he was studying here from a school's news article I found. But I wasn't sure when, or if, we'd run into each other. It's as though he's been waiting for me to show up for the last two years. There are only a few tables outside, and all of them are already taken. I consider waiting for one to open up, but it's been far too long, so I walk right up to him and say, "Is anyone sitting here?"

He glances up from his book. Strands of dark hair drift across his forehead as he blinks at me. It feels like a lifetime since we last saw each other. I'm waiting to see a flicker of recognition somewhere in his eyes, but his expression doesn't change when he says, "No. Go ahead."

I wait for him to say more, but he looks back down at his book again. It's like every memory of us is gone. Just like that. I'm a little sad at first. I remind myself this is a different version of him. In this universe, we haven't met before. So I pull out the empty seat and push the sadness out of my mind. It's still nice to see him again. Even if he doesn't know who I am.

A woman comes out to pour me a glass of water. I take a sip and think of how to start the conversation. In another timeline, I fell asleep in his bed. Now we're sitting across from each other like strangers.

To my surprise, he says something first.

"Do you live in Washington?" he asks.

I glance down at my shirt. There's a Wildcats logo on the pocket. I forgot I was wearing it. "Yeah. Born and raised," I answer.

"I live in Seattle."

"Really? I assume you're on vacation, then."

"I'm actually studying here."

"Me too. I'm taking philosophy classes at the University of Amsterdam." There are a couple of astronomy textbooks on the table. I glance at them and say, "I'm guessing you're a . . . theater major."

He laughs a little. "More or less," he says, putting his book down. "I'm actually doing research at the Anton Pannekoek Institute for Astronomy. It's also a part of the university."

"Impressive. What made you choose to study here?"

"They have an observatory with a Cassegrain telescope. It's different from others I've worked with. It's like uh . . ." He pauses to think of how to explain it.

"Like the Hubble Telescope."

"Yeah. Exactly."

"I hear it's a good time of year to see Coma Berenices," I add.

He smirks. "Is that so?"

"You know, it was named after Queen Berenice of Egypt. For sacrificing her hair to keep her husband safe during the war."

"You seem to know a lot for a non-major."

"An old friend taught me some things."

He leans back in his chair, taking me in again. "I don't think I got your name, by the way."

I smile. "Oliver. And you?"

"I'm Ben."

"*Ben*," I say, mostly to myself. "I've always liked that name."

ACKNOWLEDGMENTS

Oh, Oliver. Did you know that you would get your own book one day? Who knew throwing rocks at Julie's window would lead us to this point. I still can't believe over a million people have picked up *You've Reached Sam*. And so many readers messaged me, asking to know more about you. I'm so glad I got to write your story. Deep down, I always knew it was unfinished.

Like some of the best things in life, your story came to me unexpectedly. I was sitting in a restaurant, waiting for my friends to arrive. These friends happen to be Alex Aster and Chloe Gong. Alex was running a little late. When she finally arrived, she couldn't find our table. So I told her to meet me up front. Strangely, I didn't see her anywhere. After some texts back and forth, I decided to call her.

"I'm inside."

"I'm inside, too."

We described the same place, from the decor to the gold

letters on the door. It was the strangest feeling. *Two people standing at the exact same spot, talking over the phone, but unable to find each other.* Turns out, there was a sister restaurant with the same name. But the feeling stayed with me when we finally sat for dinner. At the end of the night, I turned to them and said, *"I know what my next book is about."*

That dinner turned into Oliver and Ben's story. So thank you to Alex and Chloe for the night that inspired it all.

As always, my next thank you goes to my sister, Vivian. The big law attorney who still finds time to read my books in their earliest stages. No matter how much time passes, we'll always be little kids sharing stories on the floor of the living room.

Thank you to my amazing agent, Jenny Bent. You truly are the best there is. Looking forward to all we have to celebrate. Of course, thank you to Molly Ker Hawn in the UK. And a lovely shout-out to Victoria Cappello and everyone at the Bent Agency.

Thank you to my incredible editor, Julie Strauss-Gabel. It's been such an amazing experience getting to work together. This book wouldn't be what it is without all you do. You truly gave new life to Oliver and Ben's story. Thank you for challenging me to perfect my writing. And thank you to the rest of the Penguin team—Anna Booth, Christina Colangelo, Jaleesa Davis, Theresa Evangelista, Rob Farren, Alex Garber, Carmela Iaria, Trevor Ingerson, Ilana Jacobs, Tracy Lakhram, Bri Lockhart, Shanta Newlin, Vanessa Robles, Emily Romero, Olivia Russo, Shannon Spann, Felicity Vallence, and Natalie Vielkind.

Thank you to Mom, Dad, Grandma, and Alvin for all the love and support.

ACKNOWLEDGMENTS

Thank you to Jack Edwards, the best friend of all best friends. I can't imagine a timeline without you in it. I'm going to convince you to move back to New York City one day. Mark my words.

Thank you to all the fans of *You've Reached Sam*. You guys truly changed my life. I hope you love this book just as much as the first.

And thank you to all my exes, even the ones that were short-lived. If you stumble across this book and think you found your name . . . no, you didn't.

DUSTIN THAO is a Vietnamese American writer based in New York City. He is the *New York Times* bestselling author of *You've Reached Sam* and *When Haru Was Here*. Dustin graduated from Amherst College with a BA in Political Science and is currently in a PhD program at Northwestern University.